# 'Not Under Oath'

## DANDY
*(Front Cover)*

Old photograph, could that be me
Back about nineteen-thirty-three?
Tha skinny, lanky, gangling boy?
My God, how well the years destroy
That childhood figure. There I was
With my first dog; helper and cause
Of many misdemeanors. Yet
Despite the years, I can't forget
Dandy: although down all those years
My dogs were myriad, still appears
Strong image in my memory
This photograph of him and me,
There on a pile of fallen leaves
Where sun-and-shadow pattern lives
In frozen magic near the door
Of an old house, that is no more.
My father wears his old tweed hat,
All out of shape from the dry and the wet,
And smokes his pipe. Lying near me now,
There is a dog. A throw-back to
That long-dead dog: for Mendel's laws
Apply to all that lives and grows;
And dogs and humans of strong strain
Repeat themselves, again, and again

# 'Not Under Oath'

## *Alfie Allen Remembers*

ALFRED ALLEN

TOWER BOOKS
1997

First published 1997 by Tower Books,
Ballincollig, Co. Cork

ISBN 0 902568 29 9

Printed in Ireland

*Front Cover*: 1933, Alfie and dog, Dandy;
standing behind, Alfie's father
and a neighbour

*Back Cover*: Alfie Allen, today, in his favourite
spot – his sitting room at Clashenure

*Acknowledgements*: I would like to acknowledge the
assistance and encouragement
of Commandant Mick Hartnett
and Mr Jerry Trant

*I dedicate this book
to myself,
because it's my turn*

# — Contents —

# — Foreword —

The publisher of this book, Pat Daly of Tower Books, has suggested that I include a short glossary of words and expressions to help out the uninitiated readers. Obvious mistakes and absurdities must of course be corrected, but certain mainly local usages and obsolete expressions will, I think, remain as they are. Those who do not understand them will get great pleasure from researching them in obscure volumes etc.

The publisher herself is Canadian-born, and still remains somewhat puzzled by our hotch-potch of Norse and Norman, Gaelic and English, and perhaps various words picked up in all the countries of Europe, Asia, Africa and Tir-na-nÓg – wherever Irish soldiers and sailors, pirates, brigands and slavers have set foot and left their genes; mainly by means of service in the British forces, but also, through soldiers serving in every army and navy in the world.

To illustrate this there is a certain obscure obscene word on a little brass plate donated by a friend of mine which remained a mystery and bone of contention between me and one other for a number of years. He maintained that it was a coinage of my own and a rather offensive one at that. Eventually however, another of our circle found it in an obsolete and offensive glossary. I then composed a short poem which correctly interpreted the verse as a clue to the riddle. It hangs on the opposite wall of the bar. For me it now is the equivalent of the Schleswig-Holstein problem. I think Gladstone said of this that only three people every understood it. Two were dead, and he himself had forgotten. My memory is even worst than his was.

# — Prologue —

## THE GREAT BARON

Who were my great contempories
Popes, Monarchs, great potentates?
Who was the Sultan in my time?
Or Cham of Tartary
Or Emperor of China
Or Shogun of Japan
When you come across them
You must look them up
But very few have to look me up
I am Munchausen, the Great Baron
Of no importance whatsoever
But I have made my own immortality
Out of my fantasies, my self-made myths
And the great glory of my deathless lies.

## A LUCKY MAN

In spite of all, I am a lucky man:
I'm seventy-two, and every single one
Of all my progeny who came alive
Into this world still lives, and is in health.
My wife is with me still, we still enjoy
Fair health: the random quirks of fate
Have fallen on us lightly; though I am
A little discommoded by my leg.
Five children, and not one a barren shoot
On our old tree; and none of our seventeen
Grandchildren with a serious fault or flaw
Of mind or body. Do I now tempt fate,

1

Boasting of my good fortune? I abase
Myself to all the gods for favours given
So far, down all the years; and pray I may
Escape the old Greek proverb; that no man
Can be called fortunate until he's dead.


## CERTIFIED

I got a letter from my bank to-day
To tell me I was dead; and they required
A cert. to that effect without delay.
Now, I admit, I feel a little tired
From time to time; but not as bad as this.
Signed by a manager it was, no less.
It is with no regret I have to say,
(That as Mark Twain remarked on seeing his
Early obituary,) that my sad end
Has been exaggerated; and so this day
Your dire certificate I dare not send;
Unless undated. Furnishing it now
Would constitute a fraud, and cause a row.


## DÉJÀ VUE

When the moon is dark, and the stars are dim;
When the roof is down in some future time;
After Apocalypse, when somebody passes
Will my ghost be there among the ashes:
There in the door where my vision showed
My ghost in the future? Will he go his road
Passing the ruin I know so well?
Or will there be nothing to see or tell?
Or even imagine, as I have done
In so many doors that I have known.

# — *Doors* —

I will never walk the roads around here again; my leg prevents it, but no matter, I can walk them in my memory. They won't be as well surfaced or even as wide in places as they are now, but my memory is in no hurry; of course, my memory also skips all the modern improvements; all those picture-window bungalows and houses inhabited by Joneses, mostly curiously placed in accordance with the taste of the planners; on hill-tops by one, and hidden carefully by his successor, who seems to think that the sight of a house will so incommode the tourists, who apparently must get the impression that Ireland is an uninhabited desert, that they will never come again. So, my memory replaces demolished houses, and restores old vistas, and even by-gone, unrepeatable clouds across the sky.

And in each doorway in each house stands a ghost. And to each ghost there is a story; some of the stories not repeatable even now, but many more of some interest. In order to make it impossible for anyone familiar with the roads and byways of this locality to positively identify any doorway. I intend to take them in no particular order of time and place. In deed many people will think they know some of the ghosts, and they may very well be right, but they can't ever be sure. So let us take to the road.

Not a trace is left of the house of the first woman that comes to mind. She is the stuff of legend; the mother of a famous British spy who worked in the Far Fast during the first World War, and she was one of the women evicted from the brothel in Farran when the Parish Priest burned it down. She appealed to the fathers of her various children, and they built her a sod house in a bit of wet waste ground, where she complained that 'the dampture of her feet went up to her heart' Here she continued to ply her trade, being known to go to the local pub, drink eight pints of porter; go home and have child and come down afterwards for eight more. She was capable of carrying a twenty-stone bag of flour or yellow meal up the hill home on her back, and once won a bet with the local smith as to which of them could drink the greatest number of glasses of porter without leaving the bar. He drank thirty-eight before nature overcame him, but she drank thirty-nine. They don't make them like that anymore.

They don't make smiths like that any more either. Once there was a forge at every second crossroads in the country. Within three miles of here there were until about fifty years ago, five, not counting my father's and my grandfather's private ones.

This story is not connected with any of those but with another one, gone for years before that to which my grandfather happened to take a horse to be shod. Now like all forges this one was a social centre. Men with little to do would find excuses to call there, and wanderers and beggars called in for the warmth and the company. Discussions went on, and on this day, by some peculiar extension of argument, a difference arose between the smith and a local farmer, as to whether the smith could crack a single louse on the anvil, with one single blow of a sledge hammer. The smith laid money that he could, and the farmer took him up on it. (This feat is not as simple as it seems, as the louse is mobile, the age-old anvil by no means an even level surface, and the face of the sledge hammer rounded and pitted with use.)

Each man having backed his fancy, a great difficulty arose; where to find a louse, country people being, in the main scrupulously clean in these matters. It appeared the bet was off. But, by great good fortune an old tramp who had come in while the discussion was in progress spoke up 'let that be no bother to ye' and plunging his hand into his armpit put, at one grasp, three lice on the anvil. The forge was cleared in an instant, and nobody ever knew who would have won the bet.

Now since ghosts have broken the bands of time, my next doorway is occupied by a man distant in time but not in place from the smith. There he is in the doorway shoulder propped against the jamb of the door, ankles crossed, cap slanted over his eyes, arms folded, fag in the corner of his mouth, loose, limber; a champion bowl player. A humorous man with a high skirl of laugh, a skillful man, handy with any kind of vehicle or tool. A sportsman adept with rod (and net) and gun and trap, to whom myxamatosis was a major disaster; a gallant man in every sense of the word, a man of parts, a judge of whiskey. A charitable Christian man, and a bit of a ruffian, God rest him. I remember him for a beautiful Irish bull, an oxymoron in fact to be pedantic, 'I never rode any woman but one

4

woman, and she was the best woman I ever rode' He was youngish when he said that.

In the 50s the village of Ballincollig was morobund. The barracks were almost empty again, having been partially rebuilt during the 'Emergency' (Our name for the greatest war in history). They had been burned during the Civil War by the Republican faction before their retreat to the fastnesses of West Cork and Kerry. No local industries had as yet been re-established, and all there was was a church, a few pubs (there are always a few pubs), a post office, one or two small shops and a police barracks inhabited by about 3 guards and a sergeant. The square was unpaved, and was inhabited by bare-footed children and half-starved mangy dogs.

My friend the rabbit-trapper's van broke down, and he had occasion to borrow my old crock of a car to get his rabbits to Cork. He was in a hurry to catch the market and, having killed one of the dogs who wandered out into the road, he drove on. I like to think that he'd have stopped for a child.

Next day his van having been repaired, his conscience began to trouble him. After all, he had been driving a borrowed car, and in the unlikely event that anyone complained about the dog, the owner of the car could be blamed for its abrupt end. He decided to call into the barracks and report the accident.

Behind the desk, writing away laboriously was a veteran guard, a good policeman; good enough to be promoted twice to Sergeant, but de-moted on each occasion through a problem with a spark in his throat that unfortunately, only large volumes of drink could temporarily extinguish.

With all that, he was an excellent policeman; perfectly able to control the young hooligans of the day with a clip on the ear and a boot up the arse, but, at the same time, taking serious crime seriously. He did not bother with trifles, indeed, when taking a crop census (a duty of the garda in those days, and done on a bicycle) he was bitten, but not severely, by one of my unlicensed dogs, while we were felling a tree without a permit. Nothing came of it.

My friend went in, full of the righteousness of a good deed and said 'Guard, I was going through the village yesterday, and I killed a dog'. 'Did you?' said the Guard. 'Tell me will you be going through it again tomorrow?' 'I will if you want me to' said my friend. 'Good' said the guard, 'Kill another one!'

5

Where to from that? Another smith I think but not as far back as the last one. A chronic alcoholic, drinking and working in alternate bursts, while his helper kept the forge going as best he could during the drunken bouts. When sober he preached temperance, and when drunk he could be offensive at times, but, once or twice when very drunk, he told me the torment that drove him to drink.

During the troubles, he, like most of the men of his time, was in the IRA The local unit took three soldiers prisoners; scarcely soldiers, band boys or something like that, three brothers, thirteen, fifteen, and seventeen years of age, who deserted for some reason. They were kept prisoners for six weeks, and the order came to shoot them, as they could identify all the local IRA members. All the members of the unit that was guarding them refused to shoot them, all except one notorious psychopath. The youngest started crying and his eldest brother slapped him across the face and said 'Die like a man.' They were buried on the spot.

The smith never got over it, especially as it was to him their parents were directed to reclaim the bodies years later.

In his final years he got worse, drinking almost continuously, and not long before he died he told me that one night in bed he had a visit from the Holy Family, and St. Joseph was smoking a pipe. I hope he is relieved of his anguish now. He was not an evil man.

The next door is a half door, and framed in it there is a woman, one of two sisters farming on their own in the hungry thirties; woman of a certain age, but never recognisable as old maids, full of spunk and humour. This was a kind of rambling house, and all kinds came there. Their brother had been a horsey man and a roaring boy before he married and left, and one of the women, the farmer when I was young, had ridden well to hounds. The other kept the house, and I can still taste her apple-cake and the Little Nora lemonade that she kept for me.

The horse-woman had been a great beauty in her youth, a flaming redhead, tall, with a good figure, a contemporary of my father's. I decline to read any more into it than that, but she was very fond of me, although she was old enough to be my grandmother and she and my father (and my mother) were very easy together always. She and her sister came to our birthdays, Christmas and Halloween parties, and I spent a lot of time in their house. My youngest aunt, the malicious one, after they were both dead threw it at me that they had been lovers. This was supposed to shock me. My attitude disappointed and disconcerted her, I said I hoped that they had been close but I doubt if it went that far. He was a deeply moral and honorable man, and then in no position to marry. Also there was the difference in religion.

She once gave me a cure for warts. Impale a snail on a blackthorn, say three Hall Marys and an Our Father and rub the warts with the snail and they'll go away. I never had warts.

Behind another half door, there is the ghost of a schoolmaster who never taught school. The house was one of these built after the big wind of 1839. Build in an excavated hole for fear of another big wind, a thatched, two-roomed cabin with mud walls and tiny windows with a half loft reached by a ladder, just like thousands of others. The schoolmaster lived there on his own. His mother and father were never married and she took the notion to go to America, handing the child in the door to his father. By great exertions and sacrifices his son qualified as a teacher, and applied for a vacancy in the local school. He was turned down by the priest as a bastard. This wasn't as bad as it sounds, because in the circumstances of the times, he would not be acceptable to people who knew all about him and the priest moved heaven and earth to get him appointed to a school many miles away. With success, but he was too proud to take it, and wasted his life doing odd jobs and weaving every year a most beautiful candlewick bedspread. These he stored one on top of the other in a large wooden chest. He was always at feud with the widow next door, a woman of enormous girth. On inspecting his chest after twenty years or so, the lower one or two, or three, being rotten with age, tore in his hands. He immediately accused the widow of coming in the window which was about eighteen inches square, and maliciously tearing his quilts.

For some imagined slight, he had fallen out with my father for some years. One day when I was about ten accompanied by some young henchmen and a dog or two, I happened to be passing his door, where he was washing his feet in a tin dish in order to pare his corns. He called me over; and out of the blue gave me ten pounds (twenty weeks pension). I didn't know what to do, and in confusion started calling a little Pomeranian pup that I had with me to go home. As she was exhausted from walking, she was already under my arm which caused him great amusement. I went home straight away and gave the money to my father. Of course he had to go and return it and the quarrel was made up. I suspect this was the object of the exercise.

At any rate he resumed his old routine dropping in around dinner time, talking to my father about anything and everything, maybe washing the car, and other small jobs. This continued until one night late we noticed there was no light in his home, and went in to find him collapsed on the floor, shiviering with cold. We got him to bed and lit the fire and made him tea. He had dropsy as it was called then (heart and kidney failure) and lasted about a week. All he wanted was a bottle of gin, which he kept in the bed and offered by the neck to anyone who came by to see him. He died happy at a good old age.

He used to make his own snuff, and at a thrashing he would gather all the buts. (No filtered fags then of course). He would peel off the papers, and crumble the tobacco into a Colemans Mustard tin, which he would roast on the range for an hour or two, when it would be ready to grind between his palms. He then had snuff, of enormous potency, for a week.

Up another long lane now to a house in ruins. Four people lived there, an uncle, his nephew, the nephew's female cousin, and a workman. I barely remember the uncle who was nicknamed 'the Dane'. I was with my father walking the farm when we met him. They had a long conversation about the weather, the crops and other items of interest. I noticed my father was careful to keep his distance, retiring gingerly as the Dane advanced to emphasise a point. As they spoke the Dane put his ash plant down his back inside his shirt and moved it vigorously up and down. My father explained later the Dane always had a large resident population of lice and fleas, and my father was keeping his distance for fear of hoppers. Whatever about that, only the Dane had any enterprise and he farmed the place well. Not so his nephew, who fulfilled his uncle's prophecy after the uncle died. He used to say 'A "measa" (with respect) boy you'll be scratching a poor man's ass yet and 'twill be your own'

After the Dane's death things went from bad to worse, and Joe lived by letting the land. Of course he never paid rates, and was always in trouble with the local rate collector, who for want of a better solution, would get some subscription from whoever took the land, so that no attempt to seize the lessee's cattle would be made. The rate collector worked on a commission, and a small bit of something was better than a large portion of nothing. However, if the rate collector could meet our hero with the rent on him, he might have a chance of an improved return in cash. This led to a curious tale.

Two brothers, old batchelors, were taking their donkey to the forge to be shod, and as they passed the local pub, they saw our hero within obviously temporarily flush of rent cash. One of them said to the other, 'I'll hop in here while you get the donkey shod, and I'll surely get the price of the shoes off your man playing cards.' However, when his brother returned from the forge, and went into the pub, the game was going sour. The price of the shoes had been doubled, and a crucial hand was about to be played, so the newcomer casually walked around the table, seeing the cards in both hands, made a gesture of despair to his brother. But his brother was equal to the occasion, for by great good fortune, a car drew up outside. Leaning forward to look out the door, he remarked casually 'The rate collector; I wonder what he is doing here' Out the back door our hero fled, forgetting the money on the table, and so shoeing the donkey.

A gradual deterioration went on over the years, and after the thatched roof fell in he lived on the wide hearth that remained; in bad weather using the Bastible oven as a toilet and going out for a drink when he had money. (Although illiterate he somehow managed to draw three pensions, an IRA one, because the local IRA admitted him to membership even though they were afraid to give him anything more deadly than the spout of a cast iron kettle, the old age pension, and a disability pension); or when broke, imposing on the neighbours for a meal. His health was remarkable and he made quite old bones in spite of all.

The man at the next gate is very vivid in my mind. A tall old man, mostly dressed in a kind of country man's uniform much used by farmers of his generation. Comprising a dark double-breasted jacket, a waistcoat, a striped shirt without collar, but with the stud in place, a brown or grey trousers, polished strong black boots, and a wide brimmed, dark hat. They always wore a strong, black, brass-buckled belt, worn if corpulent, in the manner of a Suomo wrestler under the belly, which thereby became part of the chest.

This man had no need of this subterfuge being as thin as a lath. He was eloquent and vehement and a great friend of my fathers and of mine. He is still a bright spot in the mind. A great fount of knowledge about the neighbourhood and its inhabitants, always wittily imparted, sometimes with a touch of malice to add to it. For instance, when asked the age of a contemporary of his replied 'He was always the same age as myself, but of these late years, he's only sixty-six', or his reply when told that a newly-wed bride of fifty at least was heard to boast that she wouldn't let her husband, a man of similar or greater age, into bed until he put on his pajamas. 'May the Lord wither her, when the wife and myself were married we didn't think the skin was half bare enough for us'.

He was full of Home Rule and Post Parnellite Politics and the local feuds at election times. Once when he came across three of his cousins beating a donkey with ash plants for want of available political opponents he served their purpose quite as well. His sayings were legion and after fifty years his indignation was as fresh as the day it happened. I remember him saying of a local eavesdropper that 'He'd stand in between the two cheeks of your ass for news'. In reference to a modest, unobtrusive man that he was 'like the latter end of a long drink of water', or of a very cute little man, that 'He'd mind mice at a cross of four roads' I'll never forget his reaction to the dolemen who were ordered out to save the harvest in 1947, when it rained every day for six months, and every sheaf had to be cut by mowing machine and scythe. When they were faced with the problem of making a sheaf and binding it by hand, he overheard one of them say to another 'Jack, you hold the bundle and I'll put on the band'. 'Will you get out of here before I'm up for murder, and go back to wearing grooves in yere asses up against the Courthouse corner', was his urgent request.

It is impossible to give the full flavour of the man, only those present when he had a few whiskies and a pint or two on board could fully appreciate the full colour of his stories, and the full force of his language. (Of a particularly well endowed man, that 'He had a mather on him that would beat a donkey out of a cabbage patch'.) Wherever he is now they have entertainment. He'd be an indifferent performer on the harp.

There are two men and two women in this story. Two neighbouring farmers and their wives, and a right-of-way, and thereby, inevitably, a feud. The right-of-way which gave access to part of one farmer's land, was the only entrance to the other's farm. Things came to a head, when a field of one farm was let out on con-acre to another neighbour, who when he had cut the crop, sold the straw to the enemy. He went to collect it, he was convalescing from a severe operation at the time, but that was no source of compassion. He was attacked by both man and wife, who had

10

him down and were jumping up and down on him when by great good fortune they were interrupted by a man of sufficiently powerful physique to tear them off their victim. The excuse offered for the assault was, 'I saw him coming up the lane, and I went in and blessed myself with the Holy Water, and went down to kill him'.

My next doorway is an exception that proves no rule whatsoever. In it are two women, an aunt and her niece. The aunt, a gentle woman in every sense of the word or words, her health and nerves ruined by having been a front-line ambulance driver in the First World War and only desirous of a quiet life, and the niece totally unable to give that to anyone She was the farmer, efficient, demanding, hard-working, impossible. I was the agricultural contractor that had to deal with her. She found it impossible to keep a farm labourer (or rather they found it impossible to stay with her).

Among her efficiencies was that she demanded a pre-harvest visit, so that I should be aware of when the crop would be ready, and its condition. (Confident in my Combines ability to rescue a lodged crop, she made sure of a high yield by over fertilizing to get the maximum return). The visit was really a very good idea, as it enabled me to be prepared for the worst. She had a sardonic turn of wit, as when on one such visit, striding ahead of me like a guardsman, she remarked. 'I have a very good man now Alfie, but he's gone in the wind and bad in the legs'. This was of a man whom she had never succeeded in catching idle (a tribute to the lobster-like eyes he had that enabled him to see around corners, so that he was always in gentle motion when she turned up unexpectedly.) It was no help that she was a maiden (or at best unmarried), at a difficult time of life and my distant relative.

On one memorable occasion she was favoured by a visit from a woman and her companion who had been driven from her home by a boycott brought about by her brother's arbitary execution of some innocent people in Dublin in 1916. He was adjudged to be mad, (he probably was, as all that family were mad, and he had had two years in the trenches) but that was poor consolation to the men who were executed or their families, and although she was held in enough local esteem to prevent her being shot, she got notice to quit, sold out and bought a farm in England. Some of her staff went with her. She learned tractor ploughing at eighty, and married for the first time at eighty-two. When she came, she must have been about eighty-three, as she came here and shouted up the stairs to my father who was still in bed at ten o'clock, 'Come down you're a younger man than I am' and he was about eighty-two at the time.

My father used to tell a story about a suitor who went to court her, but was deterred by what he found her doing when he arrived: she was castrating young pigs. Although he foisted this story on to someone else, I have a suspicion that it was his own. She also claimed to be a distant relative. However, my first encounter with her was when I was combining for my first distant relative. Lunch time came, the men ate in the kitchen of course as I did everywhere else, but I was summoned to the dining room. She, and her companion, a timid and spiteful woman, my host, and some others were present, I was covered in oil, dust and sweat, dressed in oily and disreputable clothes, topped off by a black beret; I preferred to keep my own council and to speak when spoken to. Lunch proceeded, the visitors had lately been infected with the bug of 'muck and mystery' farming – a primitive form of 'greens' in effect. They were around then too, and in an indirect attack on me and my fertilisers, sprays etc. – just then in the fifties becoming available – with a chorus led by her companion and others, but unsupported by my hosts, who used the same methods as I did, she loudly proclaimed the evils of modern (for the time) farming. It was unnatural. Into a pause in this diature, I made an observation, 'All farming is artificial, nature is a wilderness'.

Lunch prodeeded in silence to its silent end.


This door reveals a bachelor farmer, his working man and his elderly slattern housekeeper. She was supposed to get the meals, help with the cows in emergencies, and do the washing and cleaning such as it was.The problem was to get her out of bed in the morning. This only became crucial on a fair day, when a start had to be made as early as four o'clock to drive the cattle perhaps up to twelve or fifteen miles to a fair. She had to have breakfast, a good one, on the table before four, since they wouldn't see a bite or sup until the cattle were sold and delivered to the railway station late in the day.

They couldn't wake her, banging on her door proved to useless. So did rattling saucepans and buckets. Exasperated, they burst in her door, and there she was snoring on regardless. Cold water didn't work, and finally the farmer said, 'Catch her by the heels Jack, and we'll take her down in the yard'. They laid her down in the yard, and still she slept on.

'Jack' he said 'pull up her shirt there, and I'll throw a handfull of oats on her belly, and we'll see if the turkeys will wake her.' The farmer married soon after.

The next door has changed hands. This was about the time I was born, and the old owner was driven out by terror of invasion by night, robbery, threats of murder and so on. This was in the aftermath of the Civil War, when republican renegades were operating on their own account before law and order was re-imposed. A Protestant farmer with a wife and family, he eventually sold up and moved nearer Bandon with its greater than average Protestant population. The 'boys' tried the same tactics against my father, but while he had often had regular republican forces billeted on him during the real troubles, he refused them entry, fortified the house as well as he could, and informed them through the door that if they broke it down, he, and a friend who happened to be in the house, were armed with iron bars and hammers, and aided by the women folk would have a least two of them. They didn't care for his terms, and after firing a shot through an upstairs window, retired in good order. They mistook the crash of the commode lid my mother dropped for return fire. She was pregnant of me at the time.

But the poor timorous farmer was a much easier mark and to my father's advice to hold out, as order was being gradually imposed, replied 'That's all very well Mr. Allen, but when they put a revolver to your heart to blow out your brains, it's a different matter.'

This doorway is very out-of-the-way, and in ruins for a long life-time. This is a ghost my father knew; a ghost that had a forty year old aspiration to marriage, but who never made it. An, at least half-mad ghost, who kept two large round green stones near the hearth, and could be heard say 'come up to the fire, Mrs. Mullen' (not the right name) and carry on the two sides of an imaginary dialogue between the stones, moving them about as required. He was the object of many cruel pranks, such as pulling the chair from under him, while his heel was lodged in the look of the crane over the open fire; thereby dropping his bottom on the fire to its detriment, and routinely blocking his chimney with a bag of straw when he was out, so that when he lit the fire he had already laid before he went out he was driven out of doors by the smoke.

However, the most dangerous 'prank' was carried out by the man he had employed. A decision had been made (it was made repeatedly, but never carried out) to approach a neighbour for his daughter's hand in marriage. To further this intention, he decided to have his first and last bath. A large kettle was boiled on the heath, and without any admixture of cold water, his man poured it over him. In his struggle to escape from this, he rose, tub and all, the tub being wedged between his shoulders and his knees, and made for the door. The door being too narrow for the tub, the tub remained inside, and he fled naked and roaring into the countryside.

In this door, demolished and rebuilt stand two men who died by torture. A man and his son-in-law defended their house against intruders. The son-in-law was armed and one of the armed intruders died. This was in the lawless time during the Civil War. They were promised protection by the local IRA., but the protectors could not be found when the intruders (from outside the local area) returned for revenge. The son-in-law's gun jammed, and they were towed to death behind two cars. About six miles of rough country road did for them. It is said that the remains were thrown into an open tomb in a disused grave-yard, where dogs ate them, leaving a few scattered bones. Their screams woke all the people along the road until death relieved them.

The next doorway reveals a counter-atrocity. The local IRA commander had gone on a spree with his bodyguard. (The man who shot the three boy soldiers). They were on horseback and the gorses were tied outside the pub door. This commander (a boy of about nineteen or twenty) was, wrongly believed by the British to have been the one who shot the boys. This hadn't even happened in his area, but he was held to be responsible for it. The horses were seen by a local spy, who was never unmasked, and he reported it to the Auxiliaries, who came out in a Crosley Tender. The alarm was given and the 'bodyguard' disappeared out the window and got away on horseback across the fields. The 'body' he was supposed to be guarding wasn't so lucky, or such a practiced horseman, and just as he was mounting he was shot. No attempt was made to fight it out, even though they were both armed. His wound was not mortal, and he was towed behind the tender to the barrack some miles away. It is said that he survived even this, and (but this may be IRA black propaganda, at which both sides were highly skilled) his captors took two days to kill him, taking this and that and the other thing off him with pincers.

Just here I would like to insert a stray thought that has occurred to me. How relatively few have been our calamities, atrocities, massacres, famines, battles and general unpleasantries over the last three hundred years compared to our Continental neighbours. Since Aughrim no real set-piece battle of any scale has been fought here. Europe has been fought over in varying degrees on a big scale at least eight times and more. Huge armies have devastated Spain, France, Germany, the low countries, Italy, Austria, Russia and the Balkans, not once but repeatedly. When we speak of the famine, the reaction from Europeans must be 'What, only one major famine in three hundred years?' Even at present, our troubles, while evil and dastardly, do not bear comparision with those of Eastern Europe including the splinters of the Russian Empire and Yugoslavia. We have been relatively lucky.

However, big tragedies are only an accumulation of small tragedies, and each small tragedy is as devastating for the individual, his family and his friends as any holocaust. We can be dispassionate about calamities at a distance, for the word neighbour contains the implication of nearness, and to 'love your neighbour as yourself needs an effort of will, and assumption of responsibility that is not forced, but which comes instinctively in the case of friends or of 'neighbours' in its original meaning of propinquity. When it comes to the inhabitants of distant countries, it has to be more forced and becomes a matter of priorities; friends and the people we know must come first. Our fellow country-men before the Ethiopian, and our fellow European Christian or Jew before the fanatic Mohomedan, whose religion has no real notion of neighbourliness at all even it seems for their co-religionists (not that we Christians have done much better). Even our dog, for whom we assumed responsibility will come before any remote Amazonian cannibal. The death of a friend forty years ago, while felling a tree to bring to my sawmill, still touches me nearer than the victims of the latest earthquake or famine or war. His ghost still stands in his empty doorway for me.

This in human nature, and is therefore in an ideal world reprehensible and the cause of great suffering for humanity only exceeded by the suffering caused by idealists trying to change it, an endeavour that has always been unfortunately and disastrously futile.

15

I am now coming to a house that is no longer there, along a road, this is no longer there. I am walking back into my childhood, and if I tried it now, I would drown, for it is, except at times of extreme drought when the remains of the walls can be seen, under the waters of a Hydroelectric Scheme. In this house lived two women, a mother and daughter, who lived by knitting mainly, but they also kept a small shop, selling basic necessities. The mother was very old, and the daughter no longer young. They had some kind of knitting machine, and mother used to take them wool to be made up into socks, jumpers, pull-overs etc. The wool was our own, processed in the Dripsey or the Blarney Mills. I remember the crib in the kitchen in which a few hens resided, primitive battery hens indeed who were released to be fed when they had laid, and the eggs were collected hot and used as required. Usually they were at large in the afternoon and were fed in the yard and allowed to forage until night fall, when they returned to the warmth and light and security of the crib for fear of foxes. They talked to one another a lot, mostly I suppose about the shortage of cocks and the futility of attempting from time to time to hatch infertile eggs. Occasionally, one of them was allowed to hatch eggs obtained from a neighbouring farm where a cock was kept, and when the chickens were reared the pullets were kept for replacements, and the cocks went into the pot, as did the superannuated hens who were replaced.

The reason why I remember the women so vividly, is that they were the cause of a good beating administered to me by my father, (one of the very few and well deserved). They were so ill-advised as to give me a present out of the shop of a child's hurley and ball, and my first use of the hurley on coming home, was to drive systematically every pane of glass in the window of the room where the working men slept. I must have been a nasty little boy.

There is a house recently made into a ruin by the removal of its roof for tax reasons, as then being beyond repair, in which it is said, the front door could never be kept shut. The woman of the house used to hang her dress out of the window when her husband was away and this was the signal for her lover to come down from the hill to join her. Eventually, the pair ran away together, resulting in a lawsuit for alienation of affection and a feud between the two families. After going abroad, her beloved deserted her and married a rich widow, and she also eventually was reunited with her husband, in a vault in a local church-yard. The door of this remains shut.

Hardly any trace at all remains of the cabin down a long lane where a man my father remembered lived. He was a man of many parts, most of them bad, a cattle driver mainly employed to drive cattle to and from fairs. He kept a half-starved dog to help him, and while driving cattle to Coachford fair, the dog was being unusually dilligent to such a degree that an admiring cattle buyer offered a pound for him. At that time a pound was a considerable sum of money, and his natural avarice was aroused. If the dog was worth a pound, he was surely worth two, and no sale was made. On coming home, he sat outside the door while his wife was preparing his dinner. On the window-sill behind him was a large fresh soda-bread put out to cool. The dog came begging. A dog worth a pound at least. He started to feed a piece of the soda bread to the dog. The dog, astounded by this munificence continued to beg. Suddenly the bread was gone and the dog, starved for so long, burst, 'There I am now, with me cake ate and me dog busted, and me pound gone'.

The next door is in a ruined Cathedral on a rock. On our way to visit a friend in the far North West, we – my wife, my youngest son then about eleven years old, and myself – broke our journey to visit the rock. It was a fine Autumn day full of light and air and as we went in the Cathedral doorway which has been without a door for over two hundred years we heard the Gregorian chanting of a choir. This excited our curiosity and we looked for the source of it, a transitor radio or some recording device. The whole top of the rock was deserted. We finally traced it to the place where the choir-loft had been, above our own heads, and it finally died away. I had heard it before when I was ten on the site of an old Abbey while my grandfather was dying, one day faintly and the next more strongly both times and this later time at about three o'clock in the afternoon. Nobody but myself heard it, even though present, at my grandfather's death so many years previously, but the three of us heard it on the rock. I had no indication whose death it foretold, but I know it for the warning it was. We carried death with us to our own friend, who was even then – although still unaware of it – suffering form cancer of the stomach, which he was keeping at bay with antacid and whiskey. In spite of operations and treatment he was dead within the year. I remember his courage with pride, for he winked at me behind his wife's back when in the last skeletal stages, while she spoke cheerfully of recovery. He was a great lover and performer of music.

Which brings me to the folly and arrogance of the atheist. The puny intellect that is all that mankind has been given, is a totally inadequate tool to use to dismantle the defences of the Deity. In theory it is possible to dig the Suez Canal with a teaspoon, but how can you reach the infinity at the edge of the universe with it? We only have a teaspoon between our ears, and are all too inordinately proud of it. As for immortality, I doubt if we could bear it, yet I know, and anticipate with very mixed feelings, that the ego does survive, at least for a while, when it may be given an opportunlty to be recycled so to speak; for nature wastes nothing, all energy and mass are interchageable, going from one state to another through black holes and other as yet undiscovered devices. Why should it waste souls?

Pragmatically, I have what is for me sufficient evidence for the survival of the individual personality. I have heard the keening of the banshee four times, and always with fatal consequences. Her cry is identical with the traditional Irish keen and can only have its origin in the wailing of the dead women of the tribe for the death of a member. The dead monks sang for me also. I have also, when on the point of death, have had to drag myself back reluctantly out of the tunnel with its golden light at the end of it. If I had not had a wife and young children I would cheerfully have gone. I have seen a ghost, not visible to my father who was with me, and subsequently found that it was where a man had been killed accidently. Don't tell me that atheists have a point. It is their fear and arrogance that goads them. Agnostics? we are all really agnostics, because in the final analysis, our teaspoon is incapable of real knowledge.

This door is still the door of a family but this insignificant story comes from perhaps a hundred years ago. One of the sons of the house decided to join the RIC. When he came back his father and mother were sitting by the fire. He looked a bit crestfallen, and his father, who was a little hard of hearing, asked him how he had got on. 'They wouldn't take me at all' the son said 'I have varicose veins'. Calico veins boy, calico veins indeed. I never had 'em, maybe your mother had 'em. I never tried her.'

Another man, long vanished from his doorway put me neatly in my place with a sort of parable I suppose you could call it. I had just bought my

18

first new combine harvester, and, as he was a man of many years experience operating a Steam Traction engine and thrasher. I was demonstrating all the new means of handling grain that the combine provided, and the great economics of time and labour involved. I was full of myself. When I paused for breath, he said 'When I was a youngster down in South Cork, two penny farthing bicycles came down the road past our cottage. An old man who lived next door was standing at his gate. He turned on his heel to go back indoors, and said, over his shoulder, "I can die happy now; they can do no more".'

I had worked a thrasher myself for some years before that but with a tractor, not a steam engine. It was hard work, but it was also a kind of festival, good solid grub, and plenty of porter out of a barrel got for the occasion. Sometimes, even an extra barrel and a melodion for a dance and a booze-up the night the thrashing was done. Current soda bread was provided and 'loose mate' (sliced cold meat) and tea was plentiful, and the next day's work was often a heavy task. I remember shifting our gear one .night at four o'clock in the morning. I had two men with me. One was so drunk that we put him to sleep on top of the thrasher, and the other too drunk to walk, but he could drive the tractor. I was kind of walking wounded. We made home about six o'clock and I got two hours sleep.

Next day we pulled in to another haggard to get to work. At that time, (and at all times I suspect) there was great rivalry between young active powerful men as to who was the strongest, or the most active, or whatever. I never qualified as the most active, but I was up there with the best of them for brute strength. So was the farmer's son (whose door way now only holds his ghost, as he is dead as the result of an accident) – the majority of my contemporaries are dead now one way or another. He was filling bags of wheat while observing my dilapidated state as I skulked around the machinery with an oil can as an excuse for doing nothing. He was smiling to himself as he packed the bags with a brush-handle to fill them to capacity. Wheat is heavy and the filled sacks used at that time hold twenty stone (280 lbs), but another thirty-odd pounds could be included if the wheat was of good quality, and was packed. The wheat was of good quality. What I didn't know, but he did, was that the truck was to come soon to be loaded. The normal method of loading was with three men. Two on each side of the standing sack took hold of the bottom corners of the sack with the hand farthest from the sack and the mouth with the other. They lifted the sack and went to the back of the truck where they swung the sack in such a manner, as to put the sack bottom on the truck floor, while the third man walking behind lifted the mouth of the sack, which had sagged back, to put the sack standing on the truck floor where the driver trucked it away on his sack truck to the front of the vehicle. Two strong men by using their shoulders behind the sack, could do it on their own with great effort. There were thirteen sacks, I remember them well. My friend called me over, and said 'Give me a hand to throw these into the truck' He (and I) worked without pause, as fast as we could grip the sacks, and I can still remember the way the driver's eyes widened at our efforts. I died several times later that day.

Another door is memorable also for the man whom I remember framed in it. It was a dairy door, and in the dairy was stored the keg of porter for this man's thrashing next day – an eight-gallon keg. We pulled our thrashing set into the haggard very late, and were invited as was usual into the house. A pint of Brown Label Whisky was produced, and drunk, and the idea arose in our host's mind of tapping the barrel for a pint a man to wash it down. The usual method of doing this was not to use a tap but to bore a small hole in the end of the barrel, and drive a tapered steel punch into it. The barrel was then laid on its side up on a level stand and a bucket or large jug, was carefully drawn off by loosening the punch until porter flowed into the jug. By regulating the extent of the loosening of the punch, a head of cream could be obtained on the stout. When the jug was full, the punch would be driven home again.

There was no light in the dairy, so I shone the lights of the tractor in the door. The brace and bit were got, but the bit was blunt, and the oak barrel tough, so to obtain penetration our host mounted one of my men on his back. We drank pints a man, and pints a man again, and our host regaled us with the most scandalous stories about all the neighbours, pacing up and down the flags of his kitchen floor, his short leg the result of a badly set broken bone, causing him to undulate, so that his wide brimmed black hat cast fantastic bobbing shadows around the room. When the day dawned, the barrel was exhausted, aud another had to be got for the next (or by that time, that) day. We made our way home through the fields full of porter and scandal.

The next door held a widow and her family. One of her sons wasn't quite the full shilling, about eleven-pence-half-penny, but good-natured and harmless. A local hard man, a bully, a womaniser, happened to meet him on the road, and for the fun of it beat him up and left him stunned in the roadside drain. Walking on, the thug came to the widow's door, and called in, 'I left that fool of a son of yours back there in the drain.' The widow replied, 'Take care you wouldn't have a fool of a son of your own.' He later had two. Complete vegetables.

The next cottage was a single woman in middle life, who was amenable to suggestions about a match. A local man decided to go towards her, and an intermediary arranged a meeting in the cottage to make arrangements. Accompanied by two friends he went to his assignation. fortunately, or unfortunately, their journey involved passing a Public House They didn't pass it however without calling in for a few pints to give them heart, and arrived at the cottage, by no means drunk, but having drink taken. She made the tea for them, but her prospective husband had to excuse himself in deference to the porter. As those who know, know, once you start that you must soon repeat it. While he was away on his second errand, she turned to his friend and said 'I won't marry him at all, he has a weak bladder, and I'd be nursing him all his life'. They both married someone else, and perhaps he had a lucky escape, he got on well anyway.

The next man whose door no longer holds him, was a practical joker. He was known to have loosened the girths on the saddle of a man he had challenged to jump his horse over an awkward bank, with what could have had disastrous consequences for the rider; although much bruised and shaken, he was fortunately not gravely injured. He also removed a Lynch-pin (a pin that kept the wheel on the axle) from a laden cart that was tied up outside a pub, and took bets on how far the cart would go before the wheel fell, off, spilling the load and the driver out on the road. Again no one was actually killed, but in both cases, they might have been.
   The third instance did result in an injury. He arranged a wrestling match between two big men. Oiie of them was a big soft fool who fancied himself, and the other was a big muscular man. They wrestled for ten pounds a man. The inevitable consequence was that the hard man threw the soft man and broke his leg. They loaded him into a trap and set out for the nearest Cork hospital. However, about half way there they were tempted into a pub, and tied up the horse outside the door. After all they

had ten pounds to spend, a very large sum in those days. After about an hour or so, the publican inquired of them what was making the moaning sound outside the door. 'Ah said the joker, that's only bit of a calf that we're taking to the mart to sell him'.

On another occasion he and a neighbour celebrated the sale of the neighbour's farm by employing a man to make punch for them while they reclined in comfort, when he was heard to remark 'Hamanondial (your soul from the devil) anything less than this isn't living at all'.

This man lived up a steep winding road on the flank of a hill. From his door you could see, and be seen from a great expanse of country. A traveled man, a hobo in America during the depression, he had returned to an inherited farm, and settled down. At least he had settled down in theory, but he used from time to time to indulge in heroic drinking bouts. I had some dealings with him; an honest decent man, and his own worst enemy. I happened to meet him at one of the last local fairs; coming down the street with a big swinging stride that was somehow too big and too wide for his middle-sized build. As we met, I invited him to have a drink at the pub whose door we had just jointly fortuitously arrived at. 'Don't you see the pin' he said. (The total abstinence pioneer pin which he was wearing in his lapel) I expressed astonishment, 'The truth is the best' he said 'I found it, and it is saving me a great deal of trouble: you see, if you bought me a pint, decency would require that I should stand you one back. While I'd almost have to force the first one down, the second would go down better. If you insisted on standing again, and you would, my throat would open, and after that you could throw the barrel down there'. I'm afraid he lost the pin again.

Only animals come in and out the next man's door now these many years. He never married and for twenty-one years of his life he ran the farm with the help of a small, crabby western man. They lived a life of more or less unbelievable squalor; bread and tea, boiled spuds and bacon occasionally, washing their own shirts etc, once a week or once a month or so. The man got literally more kicks than ha'pence. Wages were sporadic, and when things improved after the 'Emergency', and farmers actually began to pay real wages to keep men from going to England, he decided he had had enough. He quit, and adding insult to injury, sued for back wages. Time went by, and some years later, on going into the local pub of an evening, I found as the only customers the working man (by that time working for me), and his former boss. The silence was deafening, so I addressed each of them in turn, and a curious kind of conversation began, a bit like, from my point of view, sitting on a three legged stool with a broken leg. Eventually, my employee, who had no real blackness in him addressed a remark to his old acquaintance. A deadly silence was the only consequence.

About a week later, he came into his dinner and announced, 'I hear old Con' (he always referred to him as Old Con) 'got a stroke and fell down in the street. All his money was stitched into his clothes. They put him in a home and he can't talk at all. 'Twould be a good time to go and see him now.'

Memory now opens doors I had forgotten
And memory's memory doors I never knew
Most of the doors are gone, the door-posts rotten
But some still stand, and surely it is true
That age refreshes childhood memories
They glow more brightly as old age comes on
While last weeks happening fades out and dies
Before the vividness of childhood's sun
Obliquely casting shadows clear and sharp
Back on our youth in startling clarity
But has this clarity a subtle warp
Are past days idealised and what if we
Remembered things much better than they were
Forget youth's agonies and come to see
All those old days as being serene and fair
A partial and a faulty memory
For we deceive ourselves more every day
In every walk of life on every road
We ever went, and so indeed I say
I don't write under oath, I swear to God.

## PHONE CALL

I was young in my dream:
Sun on a long-demolished wall,
A long-scrapped new machine
In a long-gone lean-to shed.
Then, the miracle of an unsuspected litter
Of Spaniel pups, reared in secret
By their mother, who feared their destruction.
A cunning old brown bitch, an old dead love of mine.
And her long-dead loves looked up at me;
Old enough to be capable of trust.
Ears pricked, eyes gleaming, at their first encounter
With man, their preserver and destroyer.
And I called in delight to my friend,
'Come here'. And the phone rang.
And he was dead again:
And I was old.
By far the strangest thing about my dream
Was that although it never had reality
As it exists within by brain, it yet
Entered reality as might have been
Without the interaction that we find
In dreams, of past and present. No, it was
Neither of Then or Now: but of a time
That never happened. Could it be
Part of a parallel reality?
What might have come to pass
But for my Present, in which rang that bell?
I think I may have lost a happiness
Locked in that contemporaneous Destiny.

# — Love and the Years —

## LOVE AND THE YEARS

Can love exist without mortality?
Can I adore a quite unchanging face?
How can I, when what binds my love to me
Is woven strand by strand of fickle days?

And by this constant change more constant is
Than any love for an undying God
Can ever be; for how can mortal eyes
Distinguish the Immortal from the Dead?

Indeed the love for what has always been
Turns to indifference outside of time,
Cupped in the hand of silence, rapt, alone,
Ridiculous to me, because sublime.

Love is a thing that's gathered, chance by chance,
Out of life's ever-changing random dance.


## THE CANNIBAL

Under all love and pity, millstones grind;
Mankind is but the grist the poet needs
To feed his mill. The mill-wheel of his mind
Is turned by life and living. Though he seethes

In fury at the loss, the helplessness,
The heart-ache, the compassion, and the pain
Of seeing such courage shown in hopelessness,
A cold observer comes to life again.

The millstones turn, and grind a well-loved friend:
The flour indeed is ground exceeding small:
All those we lost down all the years now blend
    To feed the poet's hunger; so that all

The hard-fought battles we have lost to Fate,
    Feed a voracious poet's appetite.


## MY MOTHER'S RHODODENDRONS

My mother's rhododendrons, one by one,
Are dying; but she won't see them anyway.
Though some had taken sick before she'd gone.
    It is some new disease, the experts say.

The ones now left are coming into flower;
A riotous blooming in a last display.
As if flamboyantly defying death's power,
Though now their leaves are browning, and come May

The leaves will fall, and so will every flower,
And then the brittle wood will have to go
To feed the flames. In that unlovely hour
I'll have to look for what will thrive and grow

To take their place; while on an Autumn fire
They'll bloom as red as any Springtime's flower.


## FIRST BUZZ

Camelias in flower outside the door
In middle-February, and one weary bee
Climbs grimly up a petal to explore
This Promised Land of honeyed ecstacy.

Her flight is weak; so weak she had to climb
The petal's rim on foot into her goal,
Her Promised Land. And only just in time;
Pollen and honey may restore her soul.

26

Will she get back into the hive again
To lead her sisters to this Spring's first feast?
Late May will bring warm sunshine after rain,
And then the hive will throb and boil and burst;

A swarm will stream into the scented air.
Pollen and nectar will be everywhere.


## THE WHITE FLAG

A struggle for survival in the sun;
A desperate duel indeed to find a place
To breed and bring up young: and only one
Could win, and so perpetuate her race.

An interloper came, and went away
Not daring to intrude on such a fight:
And I kept up my vigil, seeing the sway
Of combat on the mound: a savage sight

This struggle for supremacy. At last
One had the greater strength, and held her ground
Victorious; the other one downcast
Fled, rather flew, forsook the hard-fought mound

Of dog-shit. So the dung-fly won the fight.
The blow-fly fled in ignominious flight.


## SLAM-BANG

The old house breathes around me in the night.
A board creaks somewhere, Could that sound be mice?
Or even, God forbid, a rat up in the attic?
No, it is just the starlings that for years
Have reared their young there; and I know no rat
Could long survive their fury at his threat
To their young fledgelings. As the sun comes up
They mimic all the sounds of other birds;

And even turn their mimicry as well
On cats, and on the rumpus of young pups.
A chorus in the dawn. But in the night
The wind has died; the starlings are asleep.
In the still night a pump begins to hum.
Which one? the water-pump? the fridge?
(The heating's off) Perhaps the night-time fall
In pressure stung the air-pump into life?
This once-still house is never now at peace.
Suddenly, a door slams. Before moderiuty
Made all that noise, I often lay awake
And heard that slamming door.
What does the slammer think of all those other noises?
That have robbed his of its uniqueness in the night?


A BETTER NATURE

The dog is not ashamed like us
Of ordure, snot, or efflatus
Nor does he care, if by the way
His lust is flagrant in display.
More serious things are his concern.
We might from his example learn
To be ashamed of cowardice,
Not to betray for any price,
To venture all on love and trust,
And with calm grace return to dust.


HARD BARGAIN

Small pup, determined to survive, your forebears
Circling the fire for scraps, made a bad bargain.
Descendants twisted into arabesques, grotesque,
Long-eared, lop-eared, hairless, shaggy,
Miniscule, immense, fawning, ferocious,
But all slaves, subjected to everything
From mass dismemberment in the cause of Science,

To neutered and pampered luxury,
From companionship and mutual trust,
To a kick in passing,
From being put down, to being put out.
Small pup, was it worth it? your two-legged masters
Are, for the most part, more despicable than you;
Cleverer admittedly, they have at least three
Terrible characteristics you do not share:
A deliberate cruelty, a self-conscious shame, and a one-sided
Preoccupation with the conundrum of Eternity.


## TENTH LIFE

This wantonness of Fate I would forfend;
That the indomitable should also end;
And that the treachery of time and chance
Should shatter, as of right, this brightest lance.

Cats I can take, or leave, but your bright gaze,
Wicked and watchful, without compromise,
Held my respect. You would disdain all love,
For you and Lucifer were hand in glove.

Victor in every battle, sovereign queen,
You tholed no rivals to your feline reign,
But reared three sets of kittens every year,
Then drove them off to keep your title clear.

You lie there dead: you met your match at last.
Better to die than give another best.
Ferociously you lived and fiercely died
Your lust of battle at last satisfied.

## UNTIMELY EPITAPH

Loving is no defence against the dark,
Being but a braggart challenge to its power,
Empty as rainbow-strike that leaves no mark,
No more than does the second on the hour.

I beat my shield for this old friend of mine,
Dumb, trusting and presumptuous. This old dog
Whose eyes cloud over, and who goes again
Into that dark, prologue and epilogue

Of all that lives. What good is loving then,
When at the end of it all comes to this
End and beginning? The hard fact of pain
Must make excuse for some small gentleness

For dogs and humans; but the love of God
Comes harder, while we trample back the sod.


## LEGS TO THE SUN

A shaft of sunlight falls upon us few
Through deep-massed clouds. Our home in time and space,
Our fortunate country of the here and now,
Has an unequalled and ephemeral grace.

Though people weep and die, and wickedness,
And senseless suffering blights this flash of sun,
Yet we may search all ages, every place,
And find no time and country has out-done

This twilight of the West, where few need watch
Their loved ones dying of hunger and disease,
Where pain is being controlled, and where the clutch
Of bitter want, capricious tyrannies

And over-much belief have been released.
Why then, have discontent and hate increased?

## LOOKING BACK

What is this rattling rumpus in my head,
Old memories on the loose inside my skull,
Old thoughts, old hopes, old happiness, old dread,
The splashings out of brain-cells over-full,

Strong echoes from the Jews great mixed-up book;
Some snatches from the sayings of the wise;
Old rhymes, old reasons, old remembered luck
Both good and bad; old flights of fancy rise

Re-focussed by old age, and come to life
More vividly than ever heretofore,
Regrets much keener than the sharpest knife,
And old fulfillments that are much, much more

Than any sorrows. In the after-glow
Such memories intrude of long ago.


## ALTAMERA

I wonder will the turn of the year
Heave me off dead centre? Will the wheel
Of my mind blur-spoke again, and my thoughts cohere?
Now that we are becoming aware
Of the Chinese curse coming true,
'That you may live in interesting times',
Can I solve any of the riddles
Posed in our most interesting times?
Or do I make the poet's most arrogant mistake?
For why should those who happen
To have glibness with words
And the tricky gift of prophecy,
(For; almost exclusively, evil prognostications,) conceive
That we are some sort of super-men? We are in truth,
By and large, ordinary, ineffectual men;
Possessing an art that depends on that most mortal thing
One particular, human language. We are all
Intoxicated by an aberration; the aberration of literacy,

31

That has half petrified language; so that we can grasp Chaucer,
If only just. Of those before him, only philosopers and sages
Survive, such as Homer and the Psalmists;
Embalmed in dead speech by the invention of letters.
But where are the spendours and felicities
Of the poets of the cave-men of Altamera?
Where are their laments and love-songs,
Their philosophies and prophecies, their worship of beauty?
But Altamera's bulls and wild horses, its dancing Shamans
Still glow on the hidden walls. Painted secretly
For a lost magic; where no eye can admire them
Properly, without flood-lighting. They burn
More impressively against time than all the words
Than a million forgotten and a thousand remembered dead poets.
Just because we have more chance interconnections in the brain
And more turmoil in the mind, so that we see
All sides of everything, does that make us
Anything but failed saints and dictators?


OWLS

We have brown owls; I saw them yesterday
Sailing in silence in the Summer dusk
Made darker by the mist beside the lake,
Deep in the wood I planted, now grown tall:
Cover for nesting. Skilled at silent flight
On soft fringed feathers, owls make little sound,
No swish to warn their prey. For sixty years
I haven't seen one, let alone a pair.
I hope for owlets.
White owls I've often seen. They used to nest
In an old tree not ten yards from my bed,
An ivied stump, when I was nine years old.
They're still around, and where they build their nest
Cannot be far away. Driving through trees
Around the house, my headlights cast their shadows
Dark on dark foliage; although ghostly white

Among the trees, their shadows seem as black
As death. Do angels cast such shadows with their wings?


WINDHOVER

The kestrel's back, the wind-hanging windhover
In the high sky, hunting, telescopic-eyed;
Scouring the ground for big beetles, mice, small birds:
All in the green grass, creeping, crawling, making small hops,
Timourous of flying; hoping for warning
Of the quick plunge, the sudden strike, death falling.
Now is the time for nesting on the ruined mill wall.
Nesting, hatching, brooding, feeding young falcons of old breeding,
New seeding. Instinct succeeding.


A MISSING POEM

I've lost a poem. I've rummaged everywhere;
A poem about crows, (or rooks?) and hawks
Or falcons, and their antics in the air.
There's not a trace in any of the books

I write in; but a missing page or two
It seems I've torn cut and given away.
To whom? For what? I only wish I knew,
I'll have to start again: and though I may

Remember what I saw: the wheeling birds,
The crows in an astonishing display
Out-flying the Kestrel; of my former words
Not one remains. Of what I wrote that day

No single line is left. My inner eye
Can see the crows assert their mastery,
Taking their turns to drive him from the sky
Out-climb, out-turn him. And it seemed to me

It was for Devilment: for he was not
A threat to them at all. Was it for fun?
A joy in malice took them in pursuit?
A wicked whim to make the bugger run?


SMALL MATTERS

Going through old papers in a cardboard box
I found a note; no date, no signature.
Written, I think, some ninety years ago.
Internal evidence suggests a dying old maid
Wrote it in the last brutal agony
Of cancer of the breast. Ironic Fate
That caused a spinster's barren breast to kill.
No, it is not her will. I have her will
Meticulously detailed and well drawn up.
No, this note deals with all the little things;
The little details to be tidied up:
Where to be buried: who should have the ducks,
The pony trap and harness: ornaments
Still in the parlour, to be parcelled out:
Small debts unpaid; small sums to be collected:
The undertaker named. All this so stark:
No sentiment at all, no piety.
Everything practical: no hope, no fear.


JUNE MIDNIGHT

How many nights like this in one long life?
Perhaps a hundred, when Earth's captive moon
In gossamer shackles like a Caliph's wife
Endlessly dreams of freedom, of no sun
Tormenting darkness: where no tethered flight
Would hold her falling endlessly around
Her Master falling endlessly. This night,
So rare a night to any of our kind,
She numbers in her bleak infinity

Throwing a reflected glory at my feet
Here in June midnight. Oh, most empty, empty,
Sadness and scent of roses: Moonlight shone
On chaos, slime, and dinosaur Shine on.


## IMPACT

What, you old bitch, still queening it on high
As if he'd never swiven you at all?
Don't you feel pricking in Tranquillity,
Your maidenhead quite gone beyond recall?

You sailed so long inviolate through Earth's dark
Until his rocket rose erect to go,
And men-sperm rode upon a far-flung spark
To make you pregnant by that boor below.

Is there no end to his presumption?
What won't he dare, now he has dared to this?
Will he go whoring out beyond the Sun?
Carrying Priapus to the Universe?

While you must stay at home and rear his brat;
Whatever kind of monster that will be.
(The rest of us are worried about that:
No matter, – we will have to wait and see.)


## DOWNWIND

I know the seasons by the barley smell;
Spring is raw earth, with green spears thrusting through;
The Summer muskiness I know so well
Pervades the moon-lit dusk, scenting the dew,

When trees are all in leaf, and insect-hum
Vibrates the golden air, the feather-sheen
Of new-eared tender barley sighs, then come
Waves of that heavy fragrance from that green

35

And whispering restless sea that promises
The golden ripening, and the harvest moon,
Ducks flighting in the dusk, the harmonies
Of man and nature through the season-run.

While Winter-time can yield no better scent
A man may savour, than the barley-smell
Caught in the glass, and to our uses bent;
The scent of malt is the best scent of all.


## MELANCHOLY MAGIC

Suddenly, it's Autumn again.
The rain is no longer Summer rain.
The green is no longer Summer green.
And I heard a raven, sight-unseen.
Gold has come in, the gold of corn.
And the sun comes later each August dawn
And among the mountains each evening now
We see a more Southerly golden glow.
And the heart grows aware of the time gone past.
And we wonder will this Autumn be our last.
And we feel in late Augusts' evening chill
Each year it's more likely than ever it will.
And the beauty around us we suddenly see
Will be for others in time to be
And an Autumn sweetness of melancholy
Sinks on my spirit magically.


## ASH QUEEN

The tree that stands in front of this old house
Is dressed again in all her summer green.
Almost the last survivor of the ash,
Still regal, many-branched, an ancient queen
Courtiered by birds and bees. Unbroken still
By storm, or rottenness, or foolish men

Who itch to humble beauty and would fell
All stubborn royalty. Beneath the tree
Her casual progeny grow wild, and when
Some winter soon we'll plant them far and free
They'll be true royal heirs in loveliness
Of this survivor; and their seed will be
True to her beauty and her stateliness.
Some other fool; more transient than the tree
May sing in their green shade's serenity.


## MAINSPRING

All those long years
Asking the Watchmaker to explain
Watches to a watch:
Shouting questions
Into a deaf ear.
Yet there is a Watchmaker,
Gadgeteer, Hobbyist, Automaton,
Or something else so beyond
The triviality of watches
As to make them by rote
As the sun makes rainbows;
Depending on rain-drop,
Cornea, and spectrum,
To cause glory to arch
Across the dark sky.
Who then can deny the rainbow
Its title to immortality?

The great ache is for permanence. In corruption
We seek a stasis. We are all Atlases
Holding the world stock-still
On our shoulders. While the muscles stand
The strain of mortality, we can remain
Just as we are. When wishing for change
Not us. We must be better off
All must adapt to us. Laugh then

Fate or God or whatever, at our dilemma
That as we change we are changed
Each wiggle of the worm
Makes it a different worm
And the fire is not quenched.


## STAR OF THE MORNING

I used to think pure evil was a rare,
A seldom thing, and that most evil deeds
Happened by happenstance; and that they were
Not done in dedication, but were weeds
Not of themselves malicious: only being
The chance results of hatred or of greed,
Of love or anger. Now I know the thing
Is not that simple; that an evil deed
Can be its own true reason; that a fiend
Sits in the universe; that chaos lies
Deep in the heart of order; that the end
Of some great force is darkness. Lord of Flies
I own your greatness, but I am for life
And light, and cling to hope. Hope sanctifies
Belief in good and order. So believe
And keep your soul alive. Hope and be wise.


## A CLOSE SHAVE

I never felt the weight of Evil's power
As much in my nightmare of last night;
Sheer brutal strength, bestial and physical.
I could not close my door against its force
Even with all the strength I had in youth
Miraculously restored to what it was,
I could not hold it shut myself alone:
Indeed, the door was opening more and more.
I called for help, and Someone answered me,
Some Power that shut the door in spite of all.
The passion and the rage outside the door

Mounted to frenzy, and I felt a hate
Beyond all hate; and all around the house
I saw an eye of fire dash here and there
Trying to come in at every opening,
Then vanish. If that fiend had forced my door,
While I, unaided, strove to keep it out,
It would have had my soul forever more.


### THE WORM DIETH NOT

In some cold corner of the heart there lies
A terrible certainty, that under all
Assaults of reason and philosophies
Souls are not mortal; though the Heavens fall.

The Earth dissolves in fire, the ego is
More durable by far than guts and bones,
Than blood and brain; that when the body dies
The soul still lives among the aftertones.

How else can one explain life's sacrifice
So often seen, for love, or for ideals,
Or for the tribe, when each corpuscle cries
Out for escape, unless the heart conceals

Some certainty beyond this craven thing
Cringing from death? How else could poets sing?


### ANTICIPATION

Horned Hunters's Moon, allowing your light tonight
To glint upon the knife the captive sees
Approach him tenderly; his screams going on,
Hiccoughing into laughter with the laugh
Of the knife-wielder touching skillfully
Each nerve in mutilation: giving light

To the short orgasm of the shattered skull
Blown broken by the brain-exploding shot:
And throwing on widows' pillows wet with tears
A light to light their hateful solitude:
Indifferent Hunters' Moon.

All peaceful here,
Moonlight and sailing clouds and quiet grass growing;
While all around diverse nocturnal things
Hunt for their hunger in the age-old way.
But man alone kills for the joy of it,
A gourmet savouring terror for itself
Chaos creeps southward in this bitter land
Horned Hunters' Moon, will we too fear your light
When next you give your shadows to these fields.


RECRUITS AND VETERANS

Candles and wine: a table spread again
For forty years of memories. So we come
Again to celebration. There is pain
For those who are not here.
    still, there are some

Survivors at the feast. And all the new
Faces at this long table, are what came
of that sharp April morning. These all grew
From that beginning. So we play the game

Of life as Fate decides. Now Lu and I
Look down the table where the candles gleam
On glasses and on faces; and we try
To call to mind the starting of the dream:
The forty-year-long dream that still goes on,
A dream of life and loving, cloud and sun.

## TRADESMAN

A poet in a pastoral key,
No passion, no complexity,
No grip upon the visionary,
    Carries but little worth.

This praise of Nature's little things,
A flower, a tree, a bird that sings,
By tranquil minds with folded wings,
    Is but a scented breath.

A poet should rant, he should proclaim,
Should deepen thought. The very name
Means maker, and with every rhyme
    A poet should give birth.

A poet should release his mind
Loosed hawk upon an upward wind,
For only bloodied talons rend
    Meaning from life and death.


## DEATH OF A HOUSE

I stand in the hall of a once-great house
Now bare to the sky; and a nettle grows
Here, on the threshold, where once I met
A wicked old woman, vindictive, and set
In a bitter way; who lived and died
With her bastard brother; with nothing but pride
In the faded past of her name and race
To keep her alive in this naked place.
She came to the door, and drew me in
Away from the valley asleep in the sun,
And I drank her health in wine as sour
As her withered heart, that is now no more.
The valley below sleeps on in the sun
As it did then. The woman is gone
The house is roofless; now here is peace.
God be good to both woman and house.

## SOLITUDE

For the first time since I was born
I slept alone in this old house.
Of twenty-eight people in my clan
Not one was here, not one was close:
No wife, no child, nor grand-child either:
None of their spouses here that night.
No wind abroad to stir a feather;
Bright moonlight magicked in black and white
Three empty houses. The cloudless sky
Filled with the marvel of the moon.
Then I slept a dreamless rock-a-bye
Until the misty Summer dawn.
Then slept again in solitude;
Free of my cares, and that was good.


## GATHERING LIGHT

The snow-drops have announced that it is spring
The crocuses insists that this is true
What if the wind is east and withering
What else are springs first flowers meant to do?

The daffodils are treading on their heels
Narcissi close behind. The birds go mad
Cooing, cawing and twittering while daylight steals
More from each night, more living from cold death.

Before death takes it back; the summer lies
Before all nature,. even sluggish blood
Like mine, flows something freer when the bees
Drone in the fullness of spring. A lighter mood

May breach the winter humour in my heart
Let's say 'Let's start again' for what that's worth.

# — Old Trades & Old Tales —

Great charges are now gathering great speed in this once obscure and remote corner of the world. Even the last traces of old things, their mere residual grassed-over remains are being removed. I, myself, removed the traces of old Famine Ridges (i.e. potato-ridges, from which the potatoes were never dug, being rotten in the ground). What can only have been a retting-pond for flax has been obliterated, for linen manufacturing in Ireland started in the South, and, as a child, I remember sheets and table-cloths that I was told were made from flax grown here. (The sheets and a pair of three-branched candelabra were commonly borrowed by neigh-bours for wakes. There was a weaver living on the land, whose trade was presumably wrecked by the linen produced by the Belfast Mills. At least he did a moon-light flit from his house owing arrears of rent.

There was also two forges within a mile or so, one of which is gone for over 100 years. One curious story, of Hayes Forge which came down from my grandfather who was present as a boy, refers to an incident in this forge as previously recounted.

Shoeing wheels was also undertaken. I remember wheels being shod in the other forge, (which survived until about 40 years ago) for my father; who made his own, and for other local wheelrights. Both my grand-fathers had forges of their own, but only my maternal grandfather shod his own wheels.

The making of wheels was a highly skilled art since the selection of the woods, the seasoning of the timber, and the allowances made for assembly were all crucial. The stock or nave was turned on a lathe, or, more laboriously, a temporary axle was installed in a roughly shaped section of a log. This was rotated by a crank handle turned on the wheel-stool (a frame consisting of two parallel beams, each with two legs. The distance between the two beams could be adjusted for different operations on the wheel.) An assistant turned the handle while the turner held his gouge on a rest and reduced the stock to size. The spokes were of oak, or sometimes ash, split (not sawn) to near the right size, and finished with

43

trimming hatchet and spoke shave. The felloes usually of elm were sawn to the curve of the wheel-rim by bow-saw, or, if available, band-saw, six felloes, or sometimes seven made up the rim, each felbe taking two spokes. A special tool called a tanger, and matching bit was used on the spoke-ends to produce a cylindrical outer end to the spokes of a length about a half-inch less that the width of the felloes. The bit was then used to bore the felloes right through. Tenons were cut on the inner end of the spokes at the right angle to give a dish to the wheel, every second spoke being staggered to a greater degree so as to give a braced strength to the wheel. Mortices were then cut in the stock, every second one corresponding to the different tenons on the spokes. The felloes were held together by dowels. The wheel was then assembled, and by means of a large compass the exact diameter of the wheel was marked on the rim, allowance being made for the squeezing of the band when cooled so that all joints would be solidly tight. Surplus wood on the felloes would be chisled and planed off, and the sides of the felloes would be planed off so that all faces were flush. The wheels were then sent to the forge to be shod.

The Smiths were supplied with the required band-iron (normally 2½" x ⅜, but my father always bought 3" x ½" which the smiths disliked because it was much harder to handle). The band-iron was cut to length, allowing for lapping for welds and, by means of a jig bolted firmly to a wall, or a tree, bent to shape. The ends were then thinned to a tapered, wedge-like shape and hammer-welded at white heat using flux and heavy hammering. They were then checked for size on the wheels and heated all-over on a circular trench. A cast-iron saucer-shaped shoeing bed with a hole in the middle was then necessary into which the wheel was dropped so that the felloes met the metal bed all round. The hot band was then taken out of the fire by special hooks and dropped on. Before the wheel could take fire the bank was cooled by buckets of water. The contraction of the band then tightened all the joints between spokes and stock and felloes, and between the ends of the felloes. This was the test of a wheelright, that everything was solid and under enough, but not too much pressure. Stock-bands made of 1½" by ¼" iron were then made and shrunk on to flats turned on both ends of the stock at the time of original turning in the same manner as the main bands. The wheels were then returned to the maker for centre boring and insertion of the boxes, (tapered cast-iron centres with outside ridges to prevent then turning in the wood). This was a precise operation, as the box and its ridges had to fit exactly when hammered down and remain tight for the life of the wheel. The stock was made with a projection on the outer end all round on the circumference to secure the linch-pin (a pin which was designed to fit through a slot in the axle outside the wheel, and which had a ring on its end which could be turned down over the axle-end when the linch-pin was in place). A slot was then cut in the stock-end to allow the pin to be inserted. Both the axle of wrought iron and its boxes were the products of a foundry, and, if properly and regularly greased, out-lasted many wheels.

Red-lead paint was then applied as, indeed it had been applied to the joints before assembly, and the job was done. Making the cart was another day's, or week's work. I, myself have done this, but when my turn came, wooden wheels were being replaced by scrap car axles and wheels; much smoother on the road, and easier to pull.


## THE SOW-GELDER

Having dealt, however inadequately, with the almost extinct trade of the wheelright and his necessary adjunct the Blacksmith, I will now try to deal with an almost certainly extinct trade (or perhaps profession) that of the sow-gelder. Just like the others, an apprentice had to serve his tune to this trade to the satisfaction of his master, and submit a trial piece at the end of his apprenticeshisp.

The term sow-gelder should be self-explanatory, but to a society urbanised in decay, it is necessary to explain it.

When an old sow had passed her prime, no longer giving large litters of bonhams (and all too often eating the few she brought forth) it became necessary to dispose of her. But how? Old sows tend to be large-framed, savage and very thin from a life of starvation and with backbones as sharp as razors on which stiff bristles grew (once used for the hairsprings of watches). Such a beast was inedible, and that is where the sow-gelder came in. By removing the ovaries, he converted her into a docile, sleepy creature, no longer tearing down doors and gates and fences in search of a boar, which could by judicious feeding of waste potatoes, cabbage, etc. and buttermilk be converted into bacon, six or seven or even more cwts of fairly edible, if rather strong meat, containing great amounts of the most glorious solid, yellow fat; eminently suitable for greasing cabbage. Three months in pickle with a little saltpetre in it, and a feed of it with floury potatoes would set any man up for long cold days on the mountain or the bog. Food for heroes.

The sow-gelder had other duties; he was also an itinerant castrater of all the farm animals, pigs, lambs, calves and colts, cats and dogs, even in older times converting cockerels to capons. The skill was to prevent excessive bleeding, and still leave enough drainage to prevent infection. To ensure this, the cord could not be cut through but rather pulled and scraped along its length with the knife, to ensure clotting. All his tools had to be kept sharp and clean, and hungry dogs and cats looked forward (except in their own case) to his coming; stable-hands also anticipated the day of his arrival, since their diet, always poor, was augmented by the results of his labours, fried with onions.

Finally, after his long apprenticeship, the day came for the apprentice to receive his papers; but not until he had completed, without assistance, his trial piece; a mouse successfully castrated single-handed without excessive bleeding or death from trauma; able to run away, if rather stiffly to freedom again.

This was a severe examination to pass; as the mouse is both agile and slippery, and in the circumstances apt to nip quite painfully; while holding him with one hand, and operating with the other was a real feat of dexterity.

## HIGGLER

Does anyone know now what a Higgler was?

They're all gone now, but for the ignorant young, a Higgler was a travelling egg-buyer. His equipment was a horse and cart loaded with egg-crates, and a little available capital. He had a different route for every day in the week, and always called to the women who kept hens on the route.

He bought as cheaply as he could, and sold to the wholesalers in the towns what he couldn't sell to shops. He always tried to lend small sums of money to women when the hens weren't laying so as to have captive suppliers whom other Higglers couldn't cut in on. Many Higglers made quite good money, I knew one man that didn't. His mother held the purse-strings, and while she educated her only son after her husband died, she kept him very short.

When she died, there was what was for the time a considerable fortune. He went mad; gambling what a man wouldn't earn in a year on the turn of a card, drinking whiskey out of pint glasses, and keeping greyhounds.

One summer morning early, his neighbour heard him going past on his way home after a night's dissipation. Soon after the neighbour heard a yelping of dogs and a bleating of sheep in his field near by. He hurried out and found his sheep pinned in a corner by the greyhounds, which must have been released for a run when their owner went to bed.

Driving them off, he went to the Higgler's house and knocked on the bedroom window, calling, 'John, your dogs were attacking my sheep'. A head came out the window and said 'Jim, I think you'd better get out of sheep', and went back to bed.

Some people have a peculiar sense of humour. Long ago, near where my father was born there was a poor farmer, (farmers have always been poor) who was getting poorer through the depredations of a fox. His hens, his geese, his ducks were disappearing one by one. In his desperation he went to his neighbour, a noted sportsman and poacher for the loan of a gun. When given the double-barrelled gun, he asked for instruction on how to use it. The neighbour asked if he knew how the fox approached his yard. He replied that he knew the fox's path well enough. They worked out how he could ambush the fox on his approach, hiding behind a stone-and-earth fence. He then asked for instruction on how to fire the gun. 'Rest it on the fence', his neighbour said, 'and when the fox comes, put the butt against your nose, and pull both triggers together, just to make sure' He shot the fox, but as I said, some people have a peculiar sense of humour. He was known as flat-face for the rest of his life.


## GOATS

In my childhood goats were a very important part of the resources of the labouring man in the countryside. They grazed 'the long acre', that is the verges of the roads and were minded by one of the children or the wife of the owner. They were milked into a sweet gallon or similar container once or twice a day. Unlike a cow, a nanny-goat is milked from the rear; great care having to be taken that she did not deliver with the milk a bonus of knobs into the can giving a unique flavour to the milk. The milk was superior to cow's milk, especially for children, as it was normally free from tuberculosis and brucellosis, and nearer to mothers' milk. It had one disadvantage (is this shared by mothers' milk I wonder?) that being naturally emulsified, the cream cannot be separated, so goat's butter cannot be made. Nobody in Ireland at that time had ever heard of goat's cheese.

One goat is uncontrollable being able to climb even the slates on houses doing great damage to them, and they can eat anything – even the poisonous stalks of potatoes; therefore two goats are the minimum. These were kept coupled together around the neck; the most popular coupling being the discarded handles of galvanised buckets, bent around their necks and joined by a short length of chain. This precluded much independent action. The puck or billy goat, was a scarce animal, kept for hire by a courageous man inured to his appalling smell and cantankerous nature in a remote place If goat owners wanted kids (marvellous eating when just weaned, cooked in a bastable oven, (a large cast iron pot with a cover), over a fire of furze roots suspended from a swinging crane), while the heat was regulated by the blast of a fire-machine (a hand driven under-floor fan). However, if kids are not wanted, the nanny-goat once she has had one pregnancy (normally either one or two kids) will continue to milk, unlike a cow, which dries up naturally, within a year, if not bulled.

One might think that a valid objection to the coupling of two goats together, might be, that with such agile animals, mutual strangulation across a wall or fence would be very common. It never happened. The country people maintained that it was impossible, having often rescued goats from such a situation. The reason for this was a phenomena unique to goats; they can breathe through both ends. To strangle a goat, it is therefore necessary to block the rear end. To do this the middle finger (the largest), must be inserted. However; this is very risky, and other methods of killing a goat, involving knives, guns or bludgeons are usually employed. Nevertheless, in emergencies, it can be done. The snag is, that the friction and suction of the goat's desperate efforts to draw his or her last breath, can result in the finger being skinned, much as an eel is skinned, giving rise to infection, arising from its exposure in the goat's rectum to all kinds of malevolent germs. This, with the extreme difficulty of skin-grafts on a finger, can lead to the loss of the middle finger, which has so many uses, and can be greatly missed.

# BUTTERMILK

Sixty years ago we made butter with a horse. Once a week the accumulated cream, which came off the separator (twice a day at each milking), was tipped into a churn adapted from a large wine barrel by my grandfather. This rested lengthwise in a frame, and was turned by hand. A hole was cut in the side, and a watertight cover was fitted to this. Through this it was filled and emptied. Internally in the barrel was a shaft running through it lengthwise. This shaft was fitted with paddles or beaters arranged around the shaft. The shaft, on crude universal joints went through the wall, where it was corrected to a device called a horse-power, originally from a horse driven thrashing machine (it could accommodate six horses) which converted the circular pulling powers of a horse, through gears into the rotary power of the shaft by means of a crown and pinion gear. One horse was enough for butter-making. The barrel was turned slowly by hand while the beaters rotated the other way. Up to 400 lbs of butter could be made at a time. The butter could not be separated from the buttermilk unless the cream was sour; and this could be a difficulty in the Winter, when hot water has to be added to 'turn' it. In hot weather it might have to be churned twice a week and cold water added. The man turning the handle of the churn, knew by the change in the note of the splashing when the butter was ready, gathering first in small globules, and then into larger chunks, at which stage loud shouts were directed at the horse-driver (often frustratingly if not perversively deaf) to stop. If the butter had 'gathered' enough, the buttermilk was drained off, and replaced by water and the churn started again to wash out the remaining buttermilk. This might have to be repeated. The butter was then taken out to be washed by hand until reasonably free of water, then salt worked into it for those customers who required it salted. Some of it was weighed out in lbs. for individual customers, but the bulk of it was sold in the lump to a merchant in Cork who salted it, dyed it with saffron, and exported it (mostly to the British Navy in Malta pre-war) in tins.

Every few years, the barrel had to be renewed. For same reason, the barrels available were about a foot too long for the frame, and my father had to cut off one end and make up a new one (larger than the old one because of the taper of the barrel). This required some skill in cooperage, and some cooper's tools. He was a Jack-of-all-trades; good at most things but nothing polished about him. I learned quite a lot from him, but failed to learn to temper a chisel. I could rarely see the red and orange colours

49

change into blue on the cooling chisel which was the clue to plunge it into water. My chisels were either too soft, or to brittle. Either useless or dangerous.

During the Economic War with Britain the price of butter varied from 4 to 6 old pence a pound, perhaps a little higher in the Winter when the cows were 'gone back in the milk' and butter was scarce.

A few years ago, when reminiscing with a man who worked here at that time, he told me that when he came to work one morning, a drowned rat was floating in the vat of cream. He drew my father's attention to it. He said he didn't wonder at my father taking out the rat, but thought it was rather extremely economical to carefully hold it in one hand while running it through the other over the vat so as not to waste any cream.


## CON PLOUGHMAN

I was taught to plough by Con Ploughman
Sixty years ago. Now he is gone to God
Full of years and honour. A small man,
But none more welcome at a thrashing;
As good at the end of the day as at the start;
A tireless piece of good-humoured whipcord.
It was a day in Spring that he taught me.
He had opened a land in a bawn field
As straight as an arrow; almost as level
As the rest of the field: and I came to watch
With a child's curiosity. He gave me the handles,
And I felt the life in the ground, the hiss of soil along the board,
The crunch of small stones on the plough-share,
The thud and clink of hooves on land and furrow,
The creak of harness, the snorts of the horses,
The steam of their breath; and somewhere
A blackbird singing in a haw-thorn bush.
At the end of the furrow I learned
To throw the plough on its side
And run it idle along the headland; and then
Say 'Hup,' to the horses, and they turned

Into the furrow again on the other side;
And the share bit again. I have ploughed
Many acres since then. I am half-deaf
From the roar of the tractor; and my neck
Has a twist to the right from looking over my shoulder
And it aches, as all my joints do in wet weather,
Part of growing old. However, the Ploughman
Earned his nickname, not from that day,
Or any other day. No, it was earned in the night.
He, and his friends being merry,
Stole a plough from the forge
And ploughed the publican's green before his front door,
Quietly, in the small hours. He took the handles:
And the green was brown in the morning;
To the dancing rage of the owner.
That was how he earned the nickname of 'Ploughman'


LET SLEEPING DOGS LIE

I have nothing to do in the harvest-time;
Goodbye to the smell of hot machines,
Hot oil, harsh dust, diesel, wild thyme
Crushed in the cutting, and barley awns
In the hair, and the navel, and God knows where
Goodbye to all that, and goodbye to a life
Spanning forty-odd years. Yet, when I hear
The roar of a combine, the click of its knife,
My ears prick up, like a crippled hound
Lying in the sun, pricks up his ears
At the sound of a horn; and the distant sound
Breaks into his dreaming. For all the years
Spent in the hunt are with him still,
And he lives again the chase and the kill.
Then back to dreaming of what is gone
In a whimpering sleep in his patch of sun

# FARM CONTRACTING

When I was married my father gave me Clashenure at a cost of 10/-, plus £30 to a solicitor. This wise law is long repealed, but in 1950 it was there to encourage old farmers to hand over, and young farmers to marry. In my case, this was putting the cart before the horse, as we had decided to marry, and on making the acquaintance of my prospective wife, my father showed the enormous generosity of which he was capable. He was an old man, and the temptation to hang on to the end must have been considerable. He had his reward in seeing four of his grandchildren.

The farm was in a very run-down condition, and as I have a natural bent for machinery, which was available on hire-purchase, I got into reclaiming the land. This meant clearing and tilling it, gradually eliminating grazing animals, since the fences were broken down, and exploiting the machinery in contracting. The first machine except for 2 tractors already there was a self-propelled combine harvester. We had hired a trailed harvester for one season, the price of which was about £450, but it was slow and cumbersome and self-propelled machines became available so we bought one on my father's advice for £1,080 less £80 discount, payable £500 down and £500 after the harvest.

In spite of some snags in design, including the reliance on a electric lift for the cutting table which usually ran down the battery in laid crops. (Indeed, the first day I had it this happened rather early, as I inadvertently sat on the starting button a lot of the time. Even then I was broad in the beam). The machine also had a rather disconcerting habit of going on fire periodically, because the large petrol engine was mounted low between the main wheels, and chaff and dust and stray grains built up on the exhaust manifold in spite of regular cleaning. As the driver sat on the 20 gallon petrol tank above this arrangement, great care was taken not to allow the fire-extinguishers to remain empty for any length of time. Still, for its time, it was a grand machine, and over four years, paid for itself twice over, paid all its expenses, cut 80 acres per year for ourselves, and was sold for £625. Combines were beginning to be popular then, as they short-circuited the whole rigmarole of cutting, binding, stooking, stacking, carting, ricking and thrashing necessary up to that.

In 1951, the second year I had the Combine, I answered an ad, looking for a contractor to cut 40 acres of wheat in Ardmore, in the County Waterford. The harvest there, and up through Tipperary and the Midlands came somewhat later than with us in south Cork, and then, and

52

for some years later, Combines migrated in September and October to deal with it. Forty acres meant a cheque for £140, in 1957 equivalent at least to £4,000 today – the pay of a man for the most of a year. Ardmore was about 55 miles away, and I drove there every day, leaving about 7 a.m. and getting home about 12.30 a.m. At that time of year, work could only start about 11 a.m. when the dew had dried off, and ending about 8 p.m. when it came down again. This meant about 4 or 5 days to cut 40 acres. The crop was the best I had ever seen up to that time, although it had been sown at the end of April, after root crops had been grazed off by cattle, (black Polled Angus) which were then sold mud fat and the crop sown then. Even though that year wheat midge, a pest unheard of up to then, had affected wheat throughout Western Europe, it was still a good crop.

The farm was about 400 acres in extent, being level, near the sea, and of limestone stone in which the limestone stores could be crumbled in the hand. A local legend said its fertility was the result of the slaughter which had occurred on it, during a great battle in antiquity, but that fertilisation would have surely disappeared long since. The farmhouse was old, but a new house had been built at a cost we were told of £8,000 (about £250,000 today). The farmer was about 40, unmarried at that time, and his mother; a very interesting old woman, was still alive. Agricultural contractors then, and even now, judged the people they worked for by the standard of the hospitality they received and these were superb people, as shown by the attitude of the local people, who came in droves to help them even in the smallest matters. The old woman was a fountain of information, and the kind of person whose local, (and indeed general) folklore and knowledge should have been recorded. She and her kind are all gone now, and most of their Ireland with them.

Out in the haggards were parallel lines of large cut limestone pillars about 4' high and with tops like mushrooms over 1' in diameter. I asked the old woman about them and she said that the ricks of wheat used to be built up in them to allow cats and dogs to keep rats and mice at bay. The ricks were then thatched to be, thrashed later with flails in Winter in the barn. She told me that her grandmother had been giving birth to her last child while her husband was dying in the next room, and times were bad just then and wheat for nothing. The ricks in the haggard were unthrashed, and everybody urged her to thrash them as she needed the money no matter how little it was. She refused, and kept them for another year, when she had a second harvest. The Crimean War broke out, and the price of wheat went through the roof As the old woman said, 'We never looked back again'.

Having completed our job, and collected a cheque for £140 we celebrated the event in a pub in Ardmore with the owner of the crop, and then we started out to drive the 70 miles or so to Banteer, west of Mallow at about 1 o'clock. Seven miles an hour was the maximum speed of the Combine and it took until 3 o'clock in the morning to reach our goal, a burnt-out farmhouse and yard, where my wife managed to find us in the rain. The reason we were there was to help a fellow Combine owner to finish his contracts, as it was getting late in the year. A 14-acre field in the derelict farm had been hired by an Engineer from Cork to grow wheat. He was constructing a sewerage scheme in the nearby town of Kanturk at the time. This enterprise would have been a great success, but for the pheasants, who trampled and ate about half of it. Cutting the remainder had its moments, as he mounted the combine with his shotgun, and it was quite exciting to have a shot whiz past one's ear, and have to swerve to avoid the corpse of a pheasant. Unfortunately, this pleasant and amiable man later fell on holiday in Spain, resulting in total paralysis from the neck down, being taken for a drunk by the police, and mishandled accordingly. Pheasants, were a plague that year along the Blackwater; indeed, when we were eating our dinner in the next farm we worked in, the women of the house were trying to keep them out of the kitchen where they came in to eat chicken's food. However, at the time we were taking our revenge by eating their relations, with rabbit, bacon, chicken, cabbage and spuds.

We worked around there for a week or so, and the man who had engaged us to help him, asked me to visit his cousin's farm, where his own Combine was harvesting cocksfoot grass-seed. Leaving my own two helpers to get on with it, off we went. Coming to a Public House, I suggested that I'd buy him a drink. He pointed to his teetotaller's badge. I then asked him if he'd drink a port wine (a drink for some peculiar reason regarded as a teetotaller's drink at that time). He refused, most emphatically, and them told me why. 'When I was about 17'; he said, 'I went with a crowd of older lads to my first dance. I had a new blue suit on, and felt a bit full of myself. They took me into a pub near the hall' (No young man would face the women without some encouragements) 'but I had the pledge'. 'Try port wine; they said, 'that won't break your pledge'. 'For an

54

hour or so I drank port wine, and liked it' 'Then I felt the need to go out to the unlit toilet for a call of nature. The night air hit me, and I got what some few people get, the *cuir circe* (the Irish for hatch, as in hen) and fell in a heap on the floor in the dark and stinking toilet. A peculiarity of the hatch, is that you lose all control of your limbs and voice, but remain stone, cold sober in you mind. For four hours, every dirty bastard in that pub pissed down on me and my nice new blue suit. I will never drink port wine again.'

When the harvest was over he came to see me to pay his bill, and he was in a state of indecision and anxiety. He wanted to buy a new car, but he was afraid this would attract the attention of the Revenue Commissioners. I gave him 'On the one hand and on the other' advice.

Shortly after, the Rural Electrification Scheme having reached him, he took out the yard fuse to install a heater for a sow and bonhams. He was unmarried, and the sister who was the housekeeper being apparently not the brightest of women, saw the fuse and put it in.

He never drank port wine again; nor anything else either.

BARLEY HARVEST

The smell of barley harvest with its gold
And bitter fragrance mixed with hot-oil scent
From engines; and the feel of grain, Live-cold,
Fresh-harvested; and shorn stubbles bent,

Lined by the weight of wheels; straw disciplined
In cubes unnaturally, then firmly bound;
And hot and dusty men with faces lined
In sweat and dirt, push the machines around.

Now here is little of the green of Spring;
And little of the waving of new ears
That have been newly born, silk-feather-wing,
Caressing to the touch, the later year's

Harsh rasping beard not hardened beard to torment
Not laden with an itching, grating, dust,
But garlanded with poppies, with the scent
Of grass fresh bruised, defenceless, and with trust

55

Of beauty and fulfilment. Here we have
Only a flint-hard fruit, strong, virile, clean,
And scented with its strength: this we must save
To have again the coolness and the green.

Now let us take the ghost of it in glass,
Cool and alive, to bring Spring to the heart.
Even in Winter, when snow-flurries pass,
It makes us warm again, and keeps apart

The gloom and harshness of a Winter wind;
For by a miracle, when barley dies
It leaves a fragrant legacy behind.
Its spirit sings of Summer and blue skies,

The poppies and the feathers of the ears,
And all the loveliness of life new-born,
Soft-rippled by the winds of other years
That have been, and will be, while there is corn

And men to sow and harvest it; and earn
Its smooth exhilaration; and to keep
Seed for the future, both of men and corn.
Humanity endures while reapers reap.


FUTURE PLANNING

Is it too late to plant an Arboretum?
Perhaps, but I have already planted some
Trees of some size; mostly of common
Kinds. Or they have grown
Of themselves; because left alone
They have self-seeded. Beech, oak, ash,
Horse-chesnut, and sycamore, (sycamore is brash
And would try
To grow in your eye
If you stood still.)
I have two kinds of larch on the hill
And four

56

Kinds of spruce, and four more
Kinds of fir, and what's more
Poplar and alder, and some rare
Exotics of one kind or another.
I have inherited some old trees:
Three huge monkey-puzzles, and these
Are fertile indeed
And breed.
There were old oaks and ash and beech and sycamore and chesnut,
And to my great regret,
Old elms, now dead of disease.
But look here, what are these?
These young elms are ten feet high;
And some live, and some die.
They have come from the living root.
So, when the beetle is starved out,
Then again there will be elms about.
My fruit trees have been a failure.
Perhaps even yet, I may have time and leisure
For apples and plums; but pears
You must plant for your heirs.


SURVIVAL

The wood beside the lake is thirty-four:
Douglas and Larch, and some few ancient oaks
Pollarded long ago, and many-branched.
We planted all around them, even though
The Forestry Inspector disagreed,
And tried to make us fell them.
This led to seedling oaks, and we preserved them.
Among the Douglas Firs I noted one
The thickness of my thumb. Now Douglas Fir
In its first years, can grow six feet a year.
The Oak kept pace, and after fifteen years
Was still alive, with three leaves in the sun.
I looked for it again the other day.
It's still alive, and even has a branch;

It now is thicker than my crippled leg.
Oak is our native tree; and I maintain
Enclose a piece of ground, and keep at bay
All ruminants: and given a century
Or two, it will defeat all scrub,
All pegwood, elder, brambles, furze and bracken.
And, if the ground be good, you'll find again
An Irish wood of Oak, our native tree.


MANTLING

The sparrow-hawk was mantling on her prey
In the long lane. I had to go that way
And so disturbed her kill. She glared at me
With raptor's eyes; yellow and lambent eyes;
Implacable in their ferocity.

She tried to lift the pigeon, but could not
So flew away implaccable in hate
For my intrusion; but what joy to see
Her mastery of flight. I must surmise
What happened when I went. Did she forget

Her prey and seek another? the first kill
Was gone when I came back, but there was still
Feathers and blood, a magpie, and close by
Two hooded crows; still there, replete and wise,
Up in a tree, almost too full to fly.


ACORN

I lie here where a passing, careless bird
Dropped me in this damp shade. I wait for Spring.
I'll make my start in Spring. If I survive
The first five years, I will last centuries.
It looks as if they'll all be gone by then;
And their infernal ruminants be so reduced
Ravaged by dogs gone wolf, hunted and harried

As to be but a trifling wayward nuisance.
Then my young trees, nursed by encroaching scrub,
By briars and brambles, hawthorns, sloes, and hazels,
Peg-wood and furze, the elder, alder, bracken,
The ash and sycamore, the birch and holly,
Will creep across this ravaged land again.
So now I dare to hope, in this damp corner,
Before my last leaf falls in my last Fall,
The sacred Oaks will win this land again.


## COIN

I have in my possession an English silver sixpence which was found by a man on his knees thinning out young turnips in one of our fields about thirty years ago. If I knew the exact place now, perhaps a metal detector might find more, but since the man who found it was a painstaking man, probably there were no more. He had, according to old custom, the privilege of growing a drill or two of potatoes, turnips, cabbage, etc. for his own use, in return for whatever farmyard manure he made during the year from his hens, a pig or two, a house cow and a donkey. Finders were keepers and he got it valued at 10/- in the old money. I acquired it from his son years later in exchange for the cast-iron seat of a mowing-machine.

The coin, although considerably worn, particularly on one side, which is odd, is dated 1567. The usual Fid. Def etc. is on it, together with the head of Queen Elizabeth the First, and the Tudor Rose. It was probably lost in the late 1570s, or the early 1580s during the Desmond Rebellion; or even as late as the time of the Battle of Kinsale. In its day, it was a considerable loss, since – as you may see in one of Christ's parables as translated in the early 1600s – the pay of a man for a day was a penny. A sixpence was a week's wages, the equivalent of say £90 today at least.

How did it come to be where it was found? The place would probably have been at that time an oak wood. Most probably it was lost by an English soldier, although it is not impossible that an Irish one had obtained it as the spoils of war or loot.

But I like to think that a wounded or starving soldier died in the oak wood – common enough in the times that were in it – and became a prey of wolves and ravens. Everything about him: his arms, his armour, his clothes, and his leather boots would have melted over 400 years. Only the coin would have remained.


## SMITH

Once, long ago, there was a blacksmith somewhere in Ireland.

He could have lived one hundred, or two hundred, or four hundred years ago and could have lived anywhere within a hundred, or even two hundred miles of here, but not four hundred miles unless he had a magic forge in Atlantis. But since the story hinges on a shilling, or shillings that is unlikely. Shillings were not current here until at least the time of the Vikings. But myth is immortal and perhaps the story goes back to a forge 10,000 years ago in Atlantis, and a silver coin of Hy Brasil.

This Smith (Oisín, perhaps?) was noted far and wide for his colossal strength.

Now a certain nobleman (He must have been a nobleman for he had leisure for diversion, and moreover he possessed a shod horse) heard tell of this mighty Smith. He too prided himself on his great muscles and decided on a trial of strength with our hero. He rode for days, following the contradictory directions you usually get in Ireland. A good example of this is the directions once got in Kerry. 'That road will carry you there, and any other place you want to go'. Very true, if you think about it. Eventually he came within reach of the forge, and, dismounting, tore a shoe off his horse. He then led the horse to the forge, and ordered a new shoe.

When the shoe was made he asked to examine it. He tore it apart in his two hands and demanded a second shoe. The smith made a heavier shoe, but this suffered the same fate. The third one, made even heavier, resisted the horseman's efforts, and the horse was shod. The rider then inquired the price of the shoe, and the smith said, 'A shilling' When the shilling was handed over, he snapped it in two, and saying it was not strong enough, demanded another. This too he tore asunder, and putting the four half shillings in his pocket, made no effort to break the third, just saying, 'I think this one will do'.

This was a man of open doors. The two doors of his barn were always open, and in and out of them he practiced his hurling skill. He could keep a ball in the air indefinitely passing through the barn and hitting it alternately outside one door and then the other. Because of his great skill, it was said that the fairies recruited him to play for their local team in an away match 40 miles north of here. He made his leisurely way to the venue, played a brilliant and victorious match, and was the hero of the occasion. However, he found the prospect of a 40-mile walk home, a bit daunting and appealed to the fairies to arrange some transport. An old wooden beam of a plough was thrown away nearby, and the fairies told him that all he had to do was mount it and it would carry him home. He was strictly warned, however, that if he spoke to it, it would land on the spot, and he would have to walk the rest of the way. The plough bounded along at a great rate, and when it came to the Blackwater Valley, it gave a great leap, and cleared it completely. He could not restrain himself, and cried out 'No greim thu a sean bheim ceatha', ('Well done me old beam of a plough'). He had to walk the rest of the way home. He was a man that liked his drop (a circumstance that might have some bearing on the beam of the plough, not to mention the fairies), and he rolled home one night with a real skinful, and rolled into bed in the settle bed in the single room beside his wife who was sound asleep. In an hour or so, nature overcame him, and he sat on the side of the bed and reached under it for the vessel. The moon was shining in the half door, and by its light he saw something large and white move in the corner of the kitchen. Whisking the poe over his head, and drowning his wife with the contents, he threw it at the ominous shape, thereby killing stone dead the sow that had been brought in to farrow. To his wife's indignant tirade, all he could say was 'As God will judge me I thought 'twas a ghost'

THE FREE TRADERS

It has become fashionable lately to display reproductions of old posters and reward notices in bars, and our local has acquired a few. One in particular of the mid-eighteenth century offers £500, (an enormous sum in those days) for information leading to the capture or destruction of a smuggler's ship 'frequenting these quarters'. This could refer to many places in Irish and British waters, but undoubtedly the South-West of Ireland and Devon and Cornwall were hot-beds of smuggling.

During a conversation with a distant cousin, I learned that a mid-eighteenth century relative of us both was a noted smuggler, whose wife's family owned at that time an island in West Cork, only accessible by a causeway at very low tide which he used for his business. His name was John Splaine, and the noted show-jumper is his descendent.

Now his wife was a Cornish woman, by the name of Tressellian, and my ancestor Joshua Allen was married to her sister. According to Burke's Joshua Allen was a Commander in the Navy. It was likely that Joshua Allen commanded the smuggler's ship.

Add to all this the following facts. Cousins of Joshua owned at that time the biggest Brewery in Cork. Other relatives were shipbuilders in Cork Harbour, and John Allen who emigrated to Portugal in 1730 (and whose firm was still extant 20 years ago) had started a wine business there.

Was Joshua Allen the Captain of the ship? He would be out of the Navy on half-pay at about the right time, as there was peace. He would have come out anyway as his elder brother had died childless, and so he came into possession of Clashenure.

It was an ideal set-up. The Vintners and Brewers in Cork to dispose of the smuggled goods; the ship-builders to provide the ship; the Allens in Portugal, the remote island as a depot; the Cornish connection in France – all in the family. If he wasn't a smuggler he was extremely negligent.

There is no direct family evidence for all this. The entry in Burke's stating that he was a Naval Commander came as a surprise to me, but his son's will names a ship's carpenter as a remote heir. Since the Allen's had a tradition of shipping and trade in ships, what would be more natural for a second son than to make a career in the Navy?

Joshua's son Kyrle Allen was in his late teens when his father died, and Kyrle in turn died when his son, another Kyrle, was an infant. This could explain the paucity of family tradition.

There is however a silver teapot made from foreign silver coins found in the house after the death of the head of the household. This must have been after Joshua's death, as his son survived until 1808, and the teapot is of an earlier date. A set of coin-weights which were used to weigh foreign gold coin, (pieces of eight, Louis Dior, pistols etc.) and a list of the coins' weights for fear the weight had been reduced by carefully clipping the edges (the reason for the milled edges or modern coins) made by Dublin Castle in the reign of Queen Anne and George I and II are still in the house. These would be essential to a smuggler.

The case rests. At that time, smuggling was a hanging offense, and discretion might have deprived succeeding generations of any tradition of it. All I have for certain of Joshua Allen is the entry he made in the family Bible of his father's death in 1744, 250 years ago and a pair of Portuguese silver shoe buckles.


## NEIGHBOURS OF OLD

Once the village of Farran had many doors: a police barracks, three pubs, a brothel and fortune-telling establishment, a courthouse, a forge, a shoemaker's shop, and various cabins of various degrees of grandeur, or the lack of it. Perhaps even a bakery. There was a local hero, a man of the most prodigious strength, who once put a barrel of porter (thirty-two gallons) in a heavy oak barrel in over the side of a bin butt (a local type of heavy cart used for transporting manure, root crops and stones or any other heavy load. The bins were extra boards put on all round to increase the carrying capacity. They were about 6 feet to the top.)

This man was not a troublesome man, except perhaps during the occasional faction fight in the area, one of which was initiated by an onlooker on a convenient commanding knoll who got bored with the lack of action among the two sides drawn up at either end of the village, and lofted a stone down on one crowd or the other and then enjoying his grandstand view of the proceedings.

The hero was a quiet man in his drinking bouts, meandering up and down from one pub to the other, more and more unsteady all day long. At that time a new recruit to the RIC had just arrived in the barracks. Full of his size and strength and the methods he had been taught of how to arrest and subdue drunks and other undesirables, he was standing in the door of the barrack with the Sergeant when his zeal overflowed. He said to his superior 'Sergeant, shouldn't we arrest that man?' The Sergeant replied 'You can if you like'.

The constable challenged the hero and grappled with him. The supposedly incapacitated drunk then caught him by his collar and the ass of his pants, and threw him bodily over the roadside fence, and into a deep, wet, muddy drain, new uniform, polished boots and all. He then staggered over to where the Sergeant stood, a calm observer from the doorway, (and incidentally, a good friend and occasional drinking companion of our hero) and said 'Sergeant, if you want to arrest me don't be sending any more of them garsoons'.

In the courthouse only petty cases were heard before a bench of

63

magistrates (Justices of the Peace) made up of local men including my grandfather. There was often an element of farce attached to some of the cases, and many people of leisure, including my father, attended for the 'crack' I wish I had listened more closely to my father's accounts of some of the more ludicrous cases, but I can only cite one case with any accuracy.

Apparently, there was a row between two neighbouring houses, and in the course of it, the man of one house invaded the kitchen of the other, where the woman of the house was frying steak. In court h er cross examination went roughly as follows:

'What did he do?'

'He blew wind in the steak pan sir'.

'He blew wind into the steak pan? Where did he get the wind he blew into the steak pan?'.'Did he turn round his backside and blow wind into the steak pan?'

'He did. sir.'

I think he was fined five shillings, and half-a-crown for rendering the steak uneatable, as it would be too richly flavoured.

FOR VICKY

You're growing up very fast
Next year you'll be thirteen
And when you are grown up
The teen years in between
Will seem as in a dream

Then you'll look back in wonder
At a silly old man in his dotage
Who told far-fetched stories
Some are true, and some are lies –
And I can't tell one from the other!

# — Yuppie Flu & This & That —

## YUPPIE FLU

I ain't no Yuppie, I ain't got flu;
I'm just plain idle through and through.
I hate all joggers and fitness freaks:
When I move my carcase both grates and creaks.
All vegetarians make me sick:
I like my steaks both juicy and thick.
I only move when I have to move;
Ease and comfort are what I love
There was a time when I had to work.
It's over now: my excuse to shirk
Is the trouble I have since I broke my thigh
And shortened my leg. While I grumble and sigh
At my great misfortune, this real excuse
Is something I use and use and use.
And I sometimes think things could be worse.
They're not half as bad as this stinking verse.

Fiddlers and poets and pedlars and tinkers
Looked on their world as it was, without blinkers,
Crippled in one way or another,
By art, and insight, and greed, and hunger,
Each exacted his own revenge
On settled people, who have no range
Of thought or feeling, but sit and fester,
Each in his own little puss-filled blister.
They each had their own way of showing contempt,
In a tune, or a verse, or the way they camped,
Or the things they sold. Now the fiddler Dan,
Without use of his legs, was such a man.
Lying hidden behind a six-foot partition

In his brother's house, so that all could listen
To his jigs and reels of a Winter's night
Without being put about by the sight
Of his twisted body. So in this house
The neighbours around came to dance and carouse.
Dan vented his spleen in the only way
That his crippled, embittered, soul could display.
If the jug wasn't passed as the night went on;
If they plagued him too much for another tune;
If in any one way he felt neglected;
Then he'd lie on his back while he projected
A fountain of piss out over the top
Of the board partition: nor would he stop
Till the whole house round was besmirched and bespattered,
And the dancers and drinkers were all of them scattered.

Why is obscenity funny at all?
So what, so our nature is animal,
What's funny about it? Why should there be
A snigger in lust? when solemnity
Would seem more seemly for reproduction,
Life's most essential animal function?
And why should the wastes of what keeps us alive
Be funny or shameful? How could we survive
Without these indispensible processes?
And what virtue is there in the singleness
Of celibate people? Why are they revered
Though life-denying? Perhaps men feared
Their own animal nature above all else;
For by it we come; and when it fails
We wither too. A wise man said,
When promised eternity ahead,
That man is as a bird in flight
That plunges from darkness into the light
And warmth and life of a lighted room,
Out of and into the dark and storm
Of a winter's night. Perhaps we are
By mockery exorcising fear

66

Of the dark and storm and bitter wind
Of the night before, and the night behind.

This is a tale of a drunken party
Of men together, noisy and hearty,
Taking punch in a tavern near
A country churchyard. 'Twas many a year
Long since, and graves were shallower then,
And around the churchyard lay many a bone.
They bet one man that he would not bring
A skull at midnight, so they could sing
A song around it, and drink his health
Out of its crown. The others by stealth
Sent one of the party on ahead
To lie in wait and mimic the dead.
He wound himself in a linen sheet,
The man who was challenged to bring the skull
Went out at midnight. The moon was full.
He found his eggshell; he picked it up;
A shape appeared, and a voice said, 'stop,
That's mine.' He dropped it and seized another.
The ghost reappeard and said, 'That's my brother.'
'Though you call him up from the bowels of Hell',
Said the valiant thief, 'I'm taking his skull.
Let him follow after.' He ran like a hare
To the door of the room where the jokers were,
And gasping 'Here 'tis', he threw it down,
'The owner is after me; bugger ye run.
The house was cleared in the blink of an eye:
They tore out careless of injury.
'Twas a very long time before any of them
Forgot the joke that they played on him.

Ellen Rearour was a beautiful woman;
She came from Rearour to the west of Macroom.
A tall regal red-head, that got great attention
Wherever she went, so it's needless to mention
That MacCarey remarked her at every Fair;
And at each such occasion he'd always be there.

67

For the small wicked archer had robbed him of rest
And lodged in his vitals an arrow of lust
A middle-aged farmer, and quite well-to-do,
He approached her old father, a labourer who
Immediately siezed the chance that was given
For such a good match for troublesome Ellen.
For her fortune was not even one single shilling
And sure he'd make sure that she would be willing
To take on MacCarey; though she had an eye
On a travelling man that often passed by.
But the match was arranged, and she had to conform
To her family's wishes: sure what was the harm?
But Ellen was never resigned to her fate,
So she slept in a grain-sack on her wedding night:
And each night thereafter until he was dead
The four-bushel grain-sack stayed on her in bed.
And MacCarey had neither the charm or the guile,
Or the force or the fervour, in all that long while
To get rid of her nightshirt. They're now side-by-side
In death as in life. Her spite and her pride
Matched his failure in wooing. They lie dead as they lived
Side-by-side, not together. Indeed, it's believed
That the grain-sack that kept her from passion and pain
Went around a tramp's shoulders to keep out the rain.


SONNET WITH ADDENDUM

My fire dies down; I have not realised
My greater dreams. They will not happen now.
I had some force; too often neutralised
By sloth's great sin, which would not let me do
The things I should; but not through idleness.
A venal sin, but through perversity,
A kind of sullen, deep unwillingness
Out of a darkness born inside me.

No matter; it is now too late to change.
Like God himself, I'm only what I am.

I've left some mark; I've made some small exchange
Of vision for reality. I claim
A verse or two at least that should survive
A year or two, the greening of my grave.

I have no rhyme for death, so rear no stone.
Out of the night I came and go alone.


WHY

Three great conundrums lie in wait for us.
The first is 'Why'; ask that of God alone.
And then two 'Hows'. How did it come to pass
This monstrous sum of things: how stars have shone,

Their birth and death; what may have come before;
And what comes after: the intricacies
Of laws laid down; their subtlety and power.
The built-in seeming little things: that water is

The only substance in the Universe
That swells when it solidifies, and so
Brought life to be. This only leaves for us
The other 'How'. How did we come to know
So little and so much? If we could solve
The secrets of these 'Hows' (and we know more
Each day that passes), then we would dissolve
Into the 'Why'; and merging with that power
Become superfluous, and afterwards
Collapse creation like a house of cards.


COMPASSION

I thought compassion dead within my heart,
Worn out by too much caring down the years;
My well of tears dried up, I stood apart
From the unbearable. who motley wears

Is armoured against pity. Life at large
Holds so much horror, yields up so much pain
That I can bear it only if I purge
My soul with mocking laughter. I refrain

From an emotion that can mend the heart
That fills it with an anger against God;
Sure road to deep damnation. So we start
To sin against His goodness. Then I stood

Beside his bed; and felt his loneliness,
His bitter hurt, his helplessness and pain:
In spite of my defences; I confess
Compassion tore my angry heart again.


## CURRENT AFFAIRS

Can it be possible for men to make
A god by much believing? Perhaps faith
Can breathe reality into a myth
If men enough for long enough, invoke?

If enough worshipping brings forth a god,
Perhaps those generations that believed
Made Christ be retrospectively conceived;
By faith created the Christ crucified?

Does faith still dye the Virgin's mantle blue?
And would it fade, if all the hailing died?
Have all the gods that men have glorified
Vanished when their believers grew too few?

Or is the ghost of Zeus real enough?
Like an appliance when the current's off?

# IGNITION

Someone is giving us matches to play with
And we are not grown up
He, (She, or it or whatever) is getting more and more reckless
Exponentially. I wish He'd stop
(Or she or it or whatever) They've got away with it
So far. First it was fire and then flint
And the bow and arrow and the boomerang
And farming, and bronze and the wheel and the glint
Of gold in the cities and iron ringing
In the forges of the armourers and the skill
Of writing, and empires and organised
War and conquests, and the tramp
Of armies, and navies on the seas
And at gathering speed, knowledge: Always knowledge
And machines, and $E = MC^2$; and electronics
To point to the stars; and for what?
What is our mission? What does He (or she or it or whatever)
Mean us to become? Perhaps He (or she or it or whatever)
Has forgot.
Make no mistake, we did not discover
All these 'advances' for ourselves
For Newton or Einstein or whatever
Unknown 'genius' who invented the wheel
Was handed a match from somewhere and rummaged
By its light for the proof of his idea. But the 'invention' revealed
He had to prove correct by his labour
It was not his own idea. He, (She, or It, or Whatever)
Gave him the match, for light
It would be nice now to think the match box is empty
But it's not.


# THE FLAGS OF SUMMER

Morose of mind while Winter's gales tear down
The flags of Summer, I am restless grown
At their surrender, feeling it my own.

71

In some part living in the whirling leaves
That fall like stricken birds about the eaves,
I, purposeless, am with the same wind blown.

Stray withered images about me fly,
Voyaging the clean and wintry sky,
Masking my dreams, weakening my certainty.
As always with the falling of the year
My vision sharpens; ever more clear and clear
I feel my transience, my inconstancy.

The falling leaves are parables; they show
Us to ourselves; for as they dry and blow
So shall we wither, shrivel, and let go.
Some before others yielding to the wind,
And some tenacious, fighting to the end,
Finally falling with December snow.

What can they say to next year's buds, but 'Be
Tenacious of a dream; and constantly
Savour the sun and wind and sap of tree.
Fear not tomorrow; winter's gales have blown
On others, and will blow when you are gone
On other brothers of our canopy'

So would I also my young shoots advise,
'Live for the living; covet with jealous eyes
All sight of beauty. If you would be wise
You too should be tenacious of a dream,
Be loved and loving; strive for no God's esteem,
Nor fear no jealous God's perversities.

For all winds blow when they will blow, and we
Are but one Season's short-lived canopy
That nourishes and shades this old Earth-tree
In this one corner of one single wood,
Who's Axe-on-shoulder Forester is God,
Who plants and fells his forest constantly'

## FUSE-BOX

The first blown fuse that made the Universe,
All in an instant, so the savants say,
From nil dimensions, but of infinite mass,
Reversed that situation; so to-day

Everything flies apart: the farther off
Going faster than the near: so it appears
From any point of view. This is enough
To cloud with doubt our hopes, and raise our fears

Of some black joke. A Joker's conjuring;
Elaborately staged, with hidden laws
Built in and then let slip: a monstrous thing
Of infinite complexity. What Cause

First dreamt this dream? But now I'd like to know
Who formed the Space wherein that damn fuse blew?


## LOST INNOCENCE

Sunlight was innocent when we were young,
Even the summer sunlight had no guile,
Even at sun-set, when long shadows flung
Stretched out forever, there seemed still a smile

In its last sparkle. Now the sun goes down
In deep foreboding; and the mind goes back
To that lost innocence in that lost time
Before the shape of things began to break,

Distort, and splinter. Now the death of friends.
The loss of ancient custom, the pursuit
Of happiness, God help us, when our ends
Must justify our means, when at the root

All innocence is blighted, and when we
Become more bound by struggling to be free.

## CREATION

First there was a force before time was
Brooding thoughtless in eternity before sequence.
How it suddenly became a First Cause
Is the great conundrum.
Perhaps it had a vision of Time
And the vision was in Time, and had to have Space
To dream in. And the dream in Space became matter.
Chaotic matter made by the energy of the vision
Or dream, which then had to bring order into the Cosmos.
For the Lord of Misrule was born in the Chaos,
An inevitable by-product of the Force becoming trapped
In its own absent-minded lapse into thought.
Now the Lord of Misrule;
Being nothing but a vandal and a fool
Could cause Creation to revert
Into mindlessness again, without good or evil.
For even as Chaos is the maelstrum of total evil
So total good is inert, is nothing.
Their balance allows the Cosmos to be.
But the Force of Order become conscious is childish and lonely,
Capricious, a mocker, a black joker.
We may be his casual experiment, his black joke.
And his blunder into time may have made him mortal;
Since he is now trapped in it.
He may be suicidal. But if so, he would be long gone.
And so would we; for we cannot
Be more or less mortal than he is by one moment
Whenever he reverts to himself.


## DIALOGUE FOR ONE

Belief is necessary for survival;
Credo ergo sum;
All things hinge on soul-revival,
Death being overcome

I may change, but must not die;
The pie must hold a plum:
There mustn't be oblivion for such as I;
Belt the salvation drum.

Made in your image, Oh god on high,
Look at my symmetry and grace:
Surely, you fashioned me the apple of your eye,
Me, and the whole human race?

Why then did you leave me all on my own,
Cast out into this desert place,
The trillioneth child of the trillioneth sun,
Abandoned in time and in space?

Just a two-legged, talking, intelligent, beast,
That's all I am in the end;
Believing in less as my knowledge has increased;
Badly in need of a friend.

Why did you cultivate that apple for me?
And give it to me third-hand?
And oppress me with knowledge and with memory,
The ability to half-understand?

If the Tree of Life still blossoms in Your Garden
Must I eat of the fruit of that top?
Must I carry this thing to its logical conclusion,
And become such another as You?


ITCHY

Christmas is over; and the New Year in;
My Muse is hesitant, procrastinates,
Comes up with a nonsensical, fatuous line
Like this; and then sardonically waits

To see what I can make of it. I read
What she has prompted, and I am dismayed
At its banality: I intercede
Again, with the unhelpful bloody jade.

75

She laughs at my request, and lets me go
Quite uninspired, to find another rhyme.
By rote I do it; the result is so
Bland and forgettable, I know that I'm

Quite out of favour with the fickle bitch;
So while I itch, I cannot scratch my itch.


## AFTERTHOUGHT

Dismay must silence us: the craziness
Of our mad world strikes home: words fall away.
Satire is helpless against what's perverse.
All is absurd; bathos is here to stay.

The world spins onward into emptiness,
Its idols crumble upwards from their clay,
Staring straight onwards with a stony gaze,
Focussed on darkness in the light of day.

Break us a rainbow then across God's knee
So that His thunderbolts no more be shot
From some dimension of His timeless sea
Into our stricken world. Let God forget
All our short-comings, and His own as well,
And join us in His afterthought of Hell.


## EARTH-MOTHER

We should bury in the foetal position,
Knees up, arms crossed, head down;
Tucked in awaiting corruption,
Flesh falling away from the bone;
Not lying supine in a coffin,
Weighed down and helpless in the brown
Earth where all living things begin,
Waiting for the ceiling coming down.
The old ones knew what they were at,

Burying back in a womb;
Knowing that all living is a death;
That the tomb is a womb is a tomb.


CACOPHONY

Encisted urn
On a windy hill,
Cremated ashes
Bits of bone.

Ancient obsequies
Almost gone,
Muted murmur
Under a stone.

A rifled grave
In an age-old mound
That apes the Pharoahs,
A louder sound.

In Bru na Boyne
Mock-Pharoahs lie
Far from the Nile
And its inland sea.

Cairn on a mountain,
Hero's grave
Irish keen
On the rising wave.

Stone with ogham
Saying somebody's son,
First tuck of drum
First certain name.

Lettered headstones
Intruding in history,
Bring sharper tones
To our cacophony.

Norman effigies,
Canopied tombs,
Arms and quarterings
In vaulted rooms.

Always the unmarked
Graves of war,
Bones that hum
Under the plough-share.

Then the brazen
Confident note
Of arrogant monuments
After the rout

To Captains and Colonels
And Buccaneers,
Arrogant fanfares
That batter the ears.

And under all
The insistant sound
Of the people lying
In unmarked ground.

When famine and fever
Fill the pits,
The racket of Empire
Falling to bits.

A discordant note
Comes after the fall,
Mock-Celtic crosses
To cap it all.

The unfinished business
We can't complete
Makes hideous din
In field and street,

Where the bomb goes off
And the hate goes on,
Again the ashes
And bits of bone.


## PROMETHEUS

Here is a mystery. Why should a being
Botch-designed for the half-uses of Eternity,
Rub two sticks together to get warm
And imagine Hell?


## ZIG-ZAG

How does the lightening-flash select
The point of impact, when its speed is such
That nothing can precurse it? The correct
Distance and conductivity both touch
Exactly at the moment of release
The doctrine of God's only true elect
Lies here in nature in the thunder-voice
Here where the elements have had effect
Upon the lightening-rod. Can we erect
Such pathways of salvation? Have we choice
Of drawing God's lightening bolt. Can we attract
The shrivelling flash of a primeval grace
That shows the ghastly brilliance of God's face.


## SPIRES

Easter Sunday and the old ritual,
Less boring than the new
With-it banality. Still unconsenting
In the heart to the blood and the agony,
The pointless rigmarole of Salvation;
God should have no need of charades.
As ever, all the splinters of Christ

Hating each other; still insisting,
'I'm right and you're wrong'.
Pointing their differing spires
Towards Heaven; all divergent;
All wrong for the same reason
There is no sign-post to the universal,
And the finite presuppose the infinite.
Yet the one most terrible heresy
Is to deny all belief,
And the greatest transgression
Is to accept mortality.
For just as the spires
Are no measure of the infinite,
even so our minds
Falter in the contemplation of eternity.


THE LAST REFUGE

Ah Hibernia, I delight to see old men,
Laughter-lines crinkling faces, tanned
Under white hair of brown scalps, relaxed,
Pensioned, content: the old folks' home
A good way away as yet, confident
Of the good years of age, of sufficiency
Earned by long tedium in office or factory.
I am of their age, and I envy them at times.
No such ease for me, land rich and money poor,
Concerned for the generations after; and obligated
By the generations before; not confident
Of anything but the certainty of surprise
In everything. Perhaps Hibernia
You will surprise them even more than me
With a collapse of certainty, with a State
Bankrupt and unable to protect them,
After all their servitudes, from hardship,
From want and deprivations in the sunsets
Of lives spent in expectation of security.
Perhaps indeed. And what then?

Ah, what then, Hibernia.
What dragons' teeth have they sown?
What rough beastliness is ahatching,
Not in Bethlehem, but in Ballymun,
Or Belfast, or the Curragh of Kildare?
Anarchy, or order not to our liking.
The shot in the dark, or the volley in the morning.
These things are becoming possible, even likely,
While the old men are at ease in the sun,
Complacant at the success of their failures,
Smug in their stereotyped attitudes.
The country has lost faith in their successors,
Those protagonists of unwarranted assumptions,
Fed on false myths and legends.
Promising, promising, in pursuit of
Power for power's sake; which without decisiveness
Is merely another kind of paralysis.
Making mistakes by default, Hibernia,
Without even the virtue of error
Committed in the hope of good.
I do love to see the old men, Hibernia,
Sleepily content in the sun.
And when it comes to our turn to weep Hibernia,
My kind and their kind together,
I will get some wry consolation, old woman,
From their consternation as our world collapses.


AND ONE HEROINE

In our long list of those who made their mark
In our ironic saga. There remains
One other; Kathleen, Roseen Dubh, what-have-you,
Old Lop-Ears the farrow-eater, the Shan-Bhan-Bhoct
The feminine soul of Ireland, for Ireland is feminine,
Beautiful, capricious, faithless, cruel, a Siren,
Bewitching her children and setting them against each other
Because of her hatred of their various fathers
On account of their several rapes. Not caring

81

That but for these brutal encounters she would be barren,
Her Four Green Fields a howling place for wolves.
It seems as if she aches for desolation:
No Gael, no Dane, no Norman, Saxon, Scot: No Nation.


## REMORSE

My Advocate, sum up for the defence;
Emphasise righteousness; give benefit
Of doubt to all my faults; let each offence
Find its excuse; and count my lack of wit

As being unwitting. Minimise my flaws;
My sloth, my selfishness, my want of care.
Know only that I know, and that God knows
My depth of cowardice. Mention only where

I had some small successes. Hide away
Abuse of talent. Show my enterprise,
Such as it was. But let this blemish stay
To keep me from the infamy of lies.

Leave me one unhealed wound, deep underneath;
Leave that remorse so I can welcome death.


## HONEY
(written on the birth of the
youngest grandchild 'Maobh')

The last of the wine in the glass is the sweetest
Mil is for honey, the mead from the bees
Without fault or defect, the youngest, the dearest
Write out her initials, her name is to please,
The joy of her parents, their darling, their fairest
So here's to their honey, God keep her from ill
And keep her forever, 'Chomh milis le mil'.

## EASTER 1966

Good and Evil each alone
Are nothing, but becoming one
They are creative, and create
All things that are in mortal state:
They by their conflict chart the course
Of all that moves in the Universe:
So each must on the other call
To form the individual soul.

Christ and Iscariot bound together
Are necessary to each other.
Is this indeed the reason why
Judah's Innocents had to die?
Judah's mothers had cause to mourne
When the Bethlehem star shone;
Did they redeem with every shriek
This monstrous heirloom of the meek?

Christ is risen: yes indeed
Christ may rise: this is a deed
Possible in any age
To one in millions, saint and sage
Who believes it hard enough
That this fragile mortal stuff
Is subject to the eternal mind
That is in all our human kind.

Yet Good and Evil are but made
Like time and space, and light and shade;
Local conditions, atmospheres
That this single Universe shares;
That may be only a walnut-shell
In the hand of the Mover, and in his scale
There may be compassed in every pebble
A billion kinships of Cain and Abel.

And surely the Mover moves beyond
Our restricted horizons and is not bound
By such local conditions as Good and Evil,

Being neither conventional God nor Devil?
But quite outside and beyond our light,
As a rainbow to those who never had sight.
Yet one life in a million million lives
Draws strength from the mover's strength and contrives

To break the rules of time and space,
To conquer death, to look in the face
Of the Mover, the rainbow, with seeing eyes,
To prove once more that not everything dies.
Christ is risen: the Son of Man
Has gone to the Mover again and again
From every world of every star
Wherever the Mover's immortals are

And yet it is true that over all
The impositions of agony fall.
And why does the Mover not suspend
The murder of Innocents? And what end
Does suffering serve? The blood of Abel
Nourishes nothing but sorrow and trouble.
And why must Iscariot damn his soul
So that the Mover reach His goal?

And would not the stillness of goodness lie
Better upon Eternity
Than all the turmoil and pain and strife
That bubble and foam with the coming of life?
Christ is risen to save us all:
What if we'd never fallen at all?
What special virtue lies in the cross,
Emblem of pain and sorrow and loss?

And why did He leave to humanity
A biting sword as a legacy
And those arguments on original sin?
And on how many Angels can dance on a pin?
And all that hatred of brother for brother?
And that burning and flaying of one another?
And how can Christ be said to be human
And never have known the love of a woman?

And to never have known the smart of sin
Of ans injury done, and carried within;
Because now you never can go back
To undo what you've done, paper over the crack
In your self-esteem, when someone has passed
Out of the reach of your malice at last?
Without these fulfilments and these frustrations,
Christ is too Christlike for human relations.

But still He flogged through the Temple yard,
And the fig-tree withered. In this He was hard
On the barren. And water turned to wine.
Here He was human, if also Divine.
And what of the Magdalene washing His feet?
Sure the chronicler was discreet?
And He never so much as opened His mouth
When Pilate asked Him, "What is truth"?

When He left us a sword, He was only giving
Us back our own, for the sword is living:
And mankind will always find some excuse,
Big or little, for its use:
If not in politics or religion,
If not in language or race or nation,
Then in some other vaunted abstraction,
Mankind will follow the sword in action.

Though the sword no longer preaches salvation,
Today the patriot kills for his nation.
But this has almost run its course,
And now already it dabbles in worse.
Today the sword is between the races;
Murdering men for the shade of their faces.
Perhaps tomorrow the shape of the nose?
Or the idiom used? Or the cut of the clothes?

What remedy then does the singer find?
Only his song. He articulates mind,
And puts into form in disciplined words
All he can catch of the dissonant chords
That come from the puzzling mind of man;

Puzzled and puzzling; guess at the plan
That the Mover has, if Mover there be
Joining man with Eternity.


## EUTHANASIA

No one I know came here to-day;
It seems they all have gone away.
Oh, someone washed me, kept me clean.
I wonder did they really mean
To leave me hungry all this while?
I cannot speak, I cannot smile:
I've lived in limbo many years:
My eyes can see but have no tears.
My ears can hear. They did not say
When those who fed me went away
And took the tubes that gave me life,
One word of weariness or grief.
Abandoned here, the pain I feel
Of thirst and hunger, is less real
Than being abandoned here to Fate,
Forsaken, mad, disconsolate.
They should have looked into my face
And given me my coup-de-grace.
That deed of mercy would lie less
Hard on their souls than doing this.
Oh fate, or God, if God there be,
Have you, like them abandoned me?

# — Celebrations —

## CELEBRATION

Oh what a lovely party Secundus
Such atmosphere such drinking such feasting
Three separate visits to the vomitorium
All the best people conversing
All with theories and remedies for our predicament
The Northern Wall breached and abandoned
The half-ruined Rhine block-houses garrisonned
By a few fatalistic old soldiers
Grown grey from confronting the forests
But all that is so distant and dream-like
All accounts from the provinces are unreliable
Now that the post-houses are empty
And all roads unrepaired and perilous
Oh what a lovely party Secundus
This beautiful full-mooned Spring night
And the nightingales singing, singing
As if all things were unending
No corn next year from Egypt
No more, as our credit is exhausted
And there are too many pirates
While the desert creeps north in Africa
In famine will the people grow unruly
It would be better to go to Constantinople
But travel is no longer so easy
What with the brigands and the pirates
We would have to travel empty-handed
And rely on it not being worth their while
To cut our throats for amusement
And arrival would mean starting all over
Again, and for that we're unfitted

But oh, to be safe behind flame throwers
And walls both well-manned and defensible
At the prosperous hinge of the world
Safe, safe there for a thousand years
And such marvellous chariot racing
The social life is quite incredible
At the court of a real Imperator
But we would be nobodies, paupers
While here we have names and possessions
Ancestors who served the Republic
And then changed sides correctly
So that we have survived so far
We always made the fight adjustments
Now even being the right kind of Christian
In the garden there's a statue of Diana
That we pressed into service as the Virgin
The archaic and illegible inscription
Has been suitably renewed and altered
We never took religion too seriously
But now it is best to be cautious
For fanaticism thrives in adversity
Oh what a lovely party Secundus
All the gayer for a touch of unease
Not really like the feast of Democles
That comparison is much too far frtched
We've still got such a great deal to offer
To any new regime we'd be invaluable
We've had so much experience in running things
Barbarians have so much to learn
It would be such a waste not to use us
Indeed we have good grounds to be hopeful
That we could make a suitable arrangement
Oh what a lovely party Secundus
Tomorrow we'll go into the City
To see what can be got in the market
Some pearls perhaps or something of value
That can be easily hidden
Some little insurance for the future

And a little sharp knife for the wrists
If all else fails Secundus
Oh what a lovely party Secundus
Secundus, Secundus, Secundus


LIQUIDATION

Ah, Secundus, how nice to see you again.
I trust you are quite recovered from the party?
That dreadful party! I wasn't myself for a week.
I seem to remember becoming emotional;
I apologise if I sounded a little hysterical.
You don't remember? No harm done then.
I've been edgy lately; I must watch my drinking;
I can't hold it like I used to.
You think that the wine is rougher?
These days you can't depend on anything.
Let me show you something I just picked up,
An ace in the hole, a little something,
Outrageously expensive, but highly portable,
It will escape the notice of the tax-collector,
And so easily hidden about the person,
You follow me. A jewel of considerable value.
More than I can really afford but some comfort
In the times that are. But actually,
We shouldn't be starting at shadows.
I'm told by the highest authority
That Honorius is a resolute commander.
And if the worst comes to the worst, Secundus,
Even Alaric will hold the Empire together
If only for his own sake; for undoubtedly
Fleas cannot live without dogs. (Or should I say
That wolves cannot live without lambs?)
But that's too morbid. I'll give another party Secundus
Before the wine runs out, while money means anything.
I was in the slave-market yesterday, Secundus.
I won't go ever again if I can help it.
Such cultured people, now that Gaul is in ruins.

Provincials perhaps, but quite gentlemen really;
And the only bidders I saw were the mine-owners.
It brought to mind such dreadful possibilities.
Now what do you say to a party, Secundus?
Count you out? You're leaving? For Byzantium?
Can I come too Secundus? I can pay my share,
And we can guard each others' backs.
I'll sell off the slaves, everything,
And the house at throw-away prices;
Enough for another nest-egg.
Then hurrah for the Golden Horn!


PILGRIMAGE

Oh, Secundus, where is Byzantium the Golden?
Where do the timeless waves beat on the timeless shore?
Where is the secure Imperium The nightingales
Are mocking us with their heartlessness,
all magical beauty without substance,
Born of nothing but moonlight and the dreaming
Of their mocking magical god.
Here on the hillside among rocks
And terrors more hideous for being anticipated,
Stripped bare, bound, abject, among brigands,
Byzantium has become a nightmare, Secundus,
While we wait for the harsh morning.
What will they do with us, Secundus?
A quick knife to the throat, or a protracted
Sportive dissection to alleviate boredom?
As slaves we are worthless, Secundus,
A drug on the market in the mountains,
And in any case, brigands must travel light.
Oh, but to live is a craving, Secundus,
And I know now that I would not abandon existance
Pared down to a nubbin, without hands,
Eyes, manhood, taste, hearing, Secundus,
Just leave me the sensation of sunlight,

And just like the least vegetable,
The least leaf, the least blade of grass,
I would live in the ruin of living,
Tenacious, as flesh to bone


## ARRIVAL

Secundus, Ghosts have no grievances
No burdens, no nest-eggs, no Byzantiums
Secundus, we are free of all that.
But old friend when we solved those problems
Crow-bait on that Illyrian mountain
We were immediately stuck with another
What do we do with ourselves now?
Death is a deceiver, Secundus
Just like life, it is lacking in neatness
After there is neither hour-glass, normile-stone, nor sign-post
A sameness inhabited by the various
Accustomed to variety, now condemned
To monotony. Or can we take an initiative
Is there somewhere a door into nothingness
To relieve us of the burden of ourselves?
Or is that outlet also a deceiver
Do we go through it to another metamorphosis
On the same or a different mountain?


## THE TRADESMAN

My father's father did the joinery
Of this small travelling desk, and did it well.
Mahogany, I think, and meant to be
Always kept locked, and strictly personal.
A young man's love-sick verse, copies of songs,
Accounts of rents received and paid, strong boots
Ordered and paid for, accounts for clothes, shirts,
Powder and shot galore. This all belongs

Among the shadowy past of all my roots.
While Sherman marched through Georgia he was
Marching through heath for grouse, and bogs for geese.
I envy his simplicities. A pause
Before his daughter had it. Now come these
Show prizes for tame fowl. By measuring
I find, but cannot find, a secret thing.
An inner part's too thick; so there must be
An unlocated further mystery.

# — Epilogue —

## HOW MANY MORE?

Goodbye old book, I'll write no more in you.
I'll put you by, before you fall to bits.
I've torn out pages from you; so you show
But a gapped record, that no longer fits
Into the sequence that so long ago
Was set in motion down the fifty years
I've scribbled thoughts and plans, and so you go
Above your brothers, in the pile that rears
Itself three feet or more. Down at the bottom
Someone was scribbling I no longer know.
Can't read his writing. Yet, he must have some
Vague kinship with me: so we die, and grow.
My changing selves are only tied together
By my old bones, and memory's fragile tether.

## BACK COVER

I have been flattered by this photograph.
Let's put it in, why not, it might be me
On a good day? Let's give them all a laugh.
My friends will laugh at my self mockery.
Others will laugh at me; so there I am;
A source of merriment for all to see.
No reverence at all. A bloody sham,
A bloody fraud with a satiric eye
For all that is, relying on mockery
To blunt deep thought that is too deep for me
To make life bearable: A burnt out man;
I warm me at my ashes while I can.

93